Querencia

Querencia

Stephen Bodio

CLARK CITY PRESS
LIVINGSTON, MONTANA

Clark City Press
Post Office Box 1358
Livingston, Montana 59047

TO STEVE AND KATHE GROOMS
Letter Writers, Letter Readers

In particular, I thank Dutch Salmon for inviting us to New Mexico, Steve and Kathe Grooms for giving me access to Betsy's letters, and Jamie Potenberg for being a real and patient editor. And of course all our friends in Magdalena; without them, there would have been no story.

QUERENCIA:

The word doesn't translate. It is used in Spanish to designate that mysterious little area in the bullring that catches the fancy of the fighting bull when he charges in. He imagines it his sanctuary: when parked there, he supposes he cannot be hurt. . . . So it is, borrowing the term, that one can speak of one's "querencia" to mean that little, unspecified area in life's arena where one feels safe, serene.

WILLIAM F. BUCKLEY
RACING THROUGH PARADISE

Prologue

I don't know if I could have flown back the last time; it might have been too sharp a break for me to bear, loss added to loss. Instead we drove, the dogs and I, as we had so many times before, packed with my smallest possible kit of belongings into the yellow Datsun truck that had always carried us. Somewhere in Connecticut the engine would turn past 200,000 miles. The two spaniels sat in the passenger's bucket seat and stared out happily as I unrolled the landscape. They were purely content to be in my company, for they had been alone too much of late.

New Mexico was in the steel-trap grip of a hard winter, its usual browns frozen to iron gray. The day before I left a snowstorm, unusually heavy for the Rio Grande valley, had reduced visibility to about fifty feet. After attempting to finish a writing assignment at the Socorro library—the temporary house was far too cold to work in—I had hiked out in the chile fields leading down to the river with some incoherent idea of saying good-bye. The dogs blipped in and out of sight upwind as I attempted to face the storm, pulling the brim of my cowboy hat down over my eyes. And suddenly the air was full of wings and trumpet shrieks as the dogs ran in maddened circles beneath fifty rising sandhill cranes. They curved back over my head in the wind, almost low enough to touch, flying crucifixes as tall as men. I had never seen them so close; the storm had made them feel that the open field close to the house was safer than the coyote-haunted groves beside the big river. I felt like New Mexico was giving me a good-bye present, an offering to insure my return.

I reached Tucumcari on the high plains at dusk. The sunset was bloody, the snow hard and burnished, snow snakes hissing over the surface ahead of the wind, ten below promised that night. The motel lot where I finally stopped had only a narrow lane plowed out, one car with out-of-state plates parked near the office. The manager was a Pakistani; when he heard I was from Socorro he told me that his brother owned a motel there. I remembered it well; a couple of years before, when Betsy had broken five ribs and collapsed a lung in a horse mishap, she had stayed there rather than have to use oxygen at Magdalena's six-thousand-feet-plus.

In the morning I rolled out over the plains. I have never gotten enough of that country; it's like driving on top of the ocean. I drove right through Amarillo and stopped for the night at my friend Mike Evans' improbable yuppie mansion on the outskirts of Oklahoma City. He filled me up with single malt whiskey and asked how it felt to be heading back. *In uisquebaugh veritas*, or something; I sighed and blurted, "Hell, Mike, you know. It's all suburbs east of Amarillo."

STEPHEN BODIO

I

In the highlands you woke up in the morning and
thought: Here I am where I ought to be.

ISAK DINESEN

OUT OF AFRICA

The mountains looked far away. It was the snowiest winter in the
valley in twenty years. Drifts built up around the cottonwoods
and tamarisk, piled deep by circling winds. Juncos and sparrows
huddled in knots on whatever was the leeward side, exploding in
fifty directions at the attack of a sharp-shinned hawk. I sat at my
desk, the only piece of furniture in the house, a plank laid across
two upright tubes of red-clay chimney liner, and stared through
the picture window at the predator: thin legs, robin-sized body,
long rectangular tail, yellow irises ringing dilated, black pupils.
I'd concentrate until I could see those pupils expand and contract;
he would glare back at me, fixed, afraid to bend and eat the sparrow he clutched, half-buried, in the snow around his feet. Finally
he would give up, leap into the air, and vanish into the dusk, and
I would have to look at the mountains again. They stand on the
western horizon, above the peppered desert, ice-white and Pleistocene in the morning, a flat blue against the sky's dull red in the

dusk. A high plateau lies at their base, hidden by the foothills that mark the edge of the Rio's rift valley. I had a life up there on that plateau, twenty-six miles away, two thousand feet above, in another world. I could see the mountains there, too. We said that was why we stayed.

When we lived there, I would rise before dawn and leave the bed as quietly as possible so as not to set off an animal chorus of conflicting demands. I'd run water into the pot, and dump a few tablespoons of coarse-ground coffee into the filter, inhaling its sharp smell. I wouldn't run the grinder, which was sure to bring the house shuddering to life, with groans and whines and yammers and yaps, and, if we had a hawk in residence, screeches.

A mile outside a remote western town ("Turn right at Socorro; we're the first house on the right—it's just twenty-six miles") was far enough from others' eyes that there was no need for any but the most cursory dressing, a half-buttoned shirt over jeans, untied shoes against thorns. Still striving for silence, hissing curses if I bumped the pot, I'd sneak my still-numbed body through one of any number of random doors into the dawn, to sit on the steps or lean on the fence watching the steam boil off the coffee's black, oily surface. The first astringent sip seemed to turn up the volume and fine tune the focus.

Even before I was awake, Mag, the spaniel matriarch, would mutter from her night bedroom. In our sparsely furnished thirteen rooms, she shared the entrance hall with a tattered couch, a de Chirico lithograph, a gyrfalcon print, and two dog dishes.

"Not yet, Mag." Her daytime quarters, the guest bedroom, abutted the library in which slept Winston's Chevron, a yellow town dog and my favorite but Mag's bloody enemy. After their last encounter, which put them both into a near coma and which I broke up only by holding their heads underwater in the wading pool, they had taken to chewing any door that separated them, howling for blood all the while. Now we had to keep an entire room between them.

If I hadn't succeeded in my silence, Winnie would be raising a din. I'd go to the library in the far northwest corner to collect her. She'd swarm up onto my shoulders like some improbable hybrid of dog and parrot. I'd grab her before she bolted for the door between the living room and the front hall to raise havoc with Mag, then dump her down the kitchen steps to the dog yard where she'd make her circuit.

Meanwhile the bird dog twins, spaniels Sass and Bart, would be drumming and groaning in their kennel boxes in the dog room off the kitchen. "Wait! Quiet!" I'd go back to my coffee for a moment, although by this point the peace would be shattered and the animal chores relentless. Luna, the saluki, might be anywhere. He'd sleep on the couch or the floor or, sometimes, demand to be let out at three a.m. to sleep in the doghouse. But wherever he was he'd be making demands now, yodeling, poking with his right front paw, standing on his hind legs. "Wait, damnit!"

I'd get Winnie inside, and put her in the library for a moment with food. "Mag, outside!" Mag would run the perimeter, scattering lizards and growling at every spot Winnie had marked. While she was engaged I'd return to the library, scoop up Winnie and her food and water dishes, and carry them all to the cab on the back of the truck. The rear of the truck was fitted out as a dog pen and served as her morning quarters.

Back in. Mag in, Luna in or out, puppies out. Mag to the guest room, with food; she had to eat alone because she claimed all food as her right. Puppies in and fed. Luna out—or is it in?—and fed. At least Riley, the thirty-three-inch-at-the-shoulder Scottish deerhound-greyhound cross, had moved to Floyd's, a mile down the road. He was in training; besides, the smell of town bitches in heat had taught him to climb the six-foot fence around the dog yard.

Through the bathroom and out onto the porch, now enclosed by adobe walls and glass, to feed the pigeons in their big aviary. Then over to the hawk, who would already be making a racket. Hawk to outside perch. Check the live traps along the inside wall for mice; the rattlers in their terraria in the hawk room are hungry. Check the rattlers; make sure they're safe.

And last, a cup of coffee to Betsy, always a hard sleeper, still determinedly in bed, then back to the dining table behind the easternmost of the two identical front doors, to stare out at the jagged mountain silhouette to the south.

In the winter it would be cold, the sun's ascent unseen behind a wall of stone and gloom. The light in January was always arctic, the mysterious background to one of Audubon's darker paintings, a light from another time. Often the peaks, ten thousand feet above sea level and four above the plain, would be invisible for days at a time, decapitated by clouds. Their lower slopes, tilted planes built of pine and snow, were the impossibly detailed, etched silver-gray of old engravings. If there was a breeze you could inhale the incense of burning piñon and juniper from the town a mile upwind, strong and sweet, evocative and nostalgic. My sister from back east thought it was the scent of "Mexican cooking spices." Kit Carson said that if you ever smelled it you would return to the high villages of New Mexico as long as you lived.

Those accustomed to wetter climates know spring as a time of greenery and growth and happy animal lechery. But here, the wind blew out of the west for days at a time, sandblasting the rainless landscape, raising so much stinging damned dust I couldn't face it. On spring mornings we had to rise before the wind; two hours later we'd only venture out on the east side of the house, preferring even the musty, canine fug of the dog pen to sand in our eyes. "In the spring," Betsy once said, "Arizona blows through Magdalena on its way to Texas." Our library, in the room on the far west end of the house with the raised floor that had once been the landlady's dance studio, filled with dust so fine it filtered through the boarded doors and sealed windows.

In New Mexico, yards, at least those outside of Albuquerque's twentieth-century suburbs, are often nothing more than squares of sand, with fruit trees, rose bushes, vegetable and flower patches, cacti and dead trees festooned with blue bottles, all standing in isolated islands. Raked sand is cheap and neat and needs no water. But after our first spring we learned not to pull up the weeds, not even the fiendish, caltrop-bearing goat's heads, until after the winds dropped and stilled into the limpid furnace heat of June.

Summer was my favorite, an unexpected gift, because I had always hated its muggy lassitude back east. In southwestern New Mexico summer meant rain and relief. In June, just before the weather broke, we'd be in the grip of our only hot nights, when I'd toss and turn and mutter and thrash until I woke Betsy. A skitter of legs over my sweaty face—a dream?—would throw me bolt upright, grabbing for the light. June always brought an invasion of "Mexican bedbugs" or, more properly, cone-nosed kissing bugs, slithery three-quarter-inch hobgoblins with furtive moves and wings like the soft black ash of burnt paper. No matter how many I knocked down with thrown magazines as they helicoptered through the room, at least one would get through to pierce Betsy's fair Anglo skin with its folded proboscis and raise a watery blister two inches long on her leg.

But nothing would be there and I'd subside, watch her sleep, and think three a.m. thoughts. A solpugid, happily insectivorous but far nastier looking than the kissing bugs, would motor across the floor and I'd wish it good hunting. After another couple hours' bad dreams I'd wake up, dozy and stupid, and need coffee.

The next day, at about three in the afternoon, the western horizon would be a wall the color of lead. On the front of the wall would be little clouds, pale silhouettes of torn cotton. I'd try to remain calm; baby storms would have been skittering by for a week now, teasing the powdery earth with sprinkles and infusing the dry air with a breath of mountain pine, but nothing had happened yet. I'd go back to work.

A half-hour later, a dark blast of wind, laden with the odor of wet dust, would punch through the yard, swirling sand around the windows, rattling the panes. From the yard I'd see a wall towering over the town and know that we weren't going to have to water the asparagus again. We'd stand and inhale for a moment, stretching our arms toward the storm; then, as the hiss of a billion approaching drops bore down, we'd run. Pick up the hawk, call the dogs, slam some windows as the rain bashed in, soaking papers five feet from the sill. In the roaring cascade outside, we could not see the ground, hidden in the white smoke of atomized rebounding droplets. And then, hail—BB-sized, pea-sized—drifting in windows beside the walk; thunder, shaking the house, lightning flashing all around, a nearly simultaneous bang and flicker. We'd grin and the world would smell like water.

In an hour the rain would pass, the clouds emptying to our east, turning the low mountains between the house and the Rio Grande into slate blue cardboard cutouts. Nighthawks, wings crooked, wandered through the washed sky, beeping, diving, twanging, ascending again, while the tang of wet rabbit brush filled the air.

Was this the first of the real rains? As dark solidified, with a hint of more clouds in the starless void to the west, we'd get a sign: from all around the town, from new puddles in the arroyos and dirt cattle tanks, from sewage ponds across the weedy, dirt airstrip and deep holes under the highway bridge, would come the musical throbbing of thousands of spadefoot toads. For at least eleven months they "live" buried in the sand, resembling frogs' corpses. But if this first drenching was not an isolated spasm, the damp little monsters would burst out of the ground like ambulatory mushrooms and, for a month, take us to the sewage pond. There, our flashlights would first reveal twos and threes, then hundreds of toads. They floated spread-eagled, embedded in the milky surface like fruit in Jello, going about their ancient business, ignoring our conversation, our movements, even our bright lights. In our hands they were sticky, leathery. Their eyes were round and black at first, then, in the flash, the pupils would contract until they became vertical slits, cat's eyes in a toad's head. Sometimes the sheriff's car would roll in to check. "Don't worry," I heard him say to the radio once. "It's just Mansell with Bodio and Betsy, playing with frogs."

I feel as though I spent a lifetime of such summers, though there were only seven. The dawns were lush and sweet, the early skies scrubbed and cloudless before the afternoon's gathering thunder. We'd sleep well, morning and night, and make love in shaded rooms. Meadowlarks whistled atop the cholla, and blue quail cackled their repetitions from our fence posts. The walls were alive with lizards, and the bare sand erupted with spiny green growth. Even the coyotes became a little careless in this safe time. Sometimes we'd see one hurrying through the rabbit brush an hour or more from darkness. I would stand outside for hours, looking, not really goofing off, knowing I should go in soon and do whatever was necessary for my work.

On summer evenings, the stucco walls were lit with orange light from the west, washed by gold rain. When we ate in Floyd's backyard a sort of alpenglow lingered on the west-facing mountain wall over the village, showing details as sharp as those under a magnifying glass, only red, glowing brighter than the dark-blue sky. We'd sit on folding chairs, moving often to avoid the circling smoke, and fill our bellies with stew of lamb or *cabrito*, simmered for hours with tomatoes, potatoes and maybe hot chiles in a Dutch oven in the campfire pit behind the trailer house. The big sighthounds would amble about in their stiff-legged way, thrusting blunt heads against us to be petted. Game hens, brown and slick and as wild as junglefowl, would step about, then clap up into the bare trees, silhouetting their roosting bulk against the night. The talk—of Indians and animals, past times and the vast land-scape—would slow and pause, and finally subside. In the evening's last silent moments our whole world would be red coals and pinprick stars and, as we rose, a breath of wind to push away the fragrant, clinging smoke.

I might have loved summer best, but I was always susceptible to fall's conventional glories. New Mexico's high-country autumn seemed to start in August and carry on forever. Summer was for work, in long shifts and into the evening, for catfish in the Rio, for the Old Timer's Fiesta and the fiestas at Kelly and Magdalena and Santa Rita. December was for feasting and serious sit-down drinking, for travel and family, and January for torpor and rest before spring's brooding and summer's renewal. But fall was for adventure.

In fall the mornings were cold and luminous and full of antic-ipation. At breakfast we were always hungry, eating bacon and wild-pig sausage, kidneys, chicken livers with rosemary, eggs and black coffee and real tea and fresh fruit, French toast and English muffins and bagels and lox. We'd each bring books to the table, also the Albuquerque *Journal*, any of twenty-five magazines we subscribed to, new things and old favorites like Tom McGuane and Evelyn Waugh, perhaps the Socorro *Defensor Chieftain*, a weekly Betsy wrote for. If one of us had been out early, there'd be mail, perhaps a letter from a friend or from England or the family, maybe even a check. We'd eat and read, to ourselves and aloud, make notes, share items ("There's been another jailbreak at Los Lunas; is that the third or the fourth this month?"), run back into the kitchen to make more coffee or tea or toast, and plot and plan. We could "waste"—I do not use this word now—two hours this way, laughing amidst the debris of food and mail, running up the phone bills as we answered letters and wove more lines in our intricate web of communications. Finally we would force ourselves to an hour's work. Betsy would chain herself to her tape-powered Model T of a word processor in her room, an oasis of disorder in an otherwise reasonably neat house. ("I can't find your letter," I once heard her complain to an editor, "Stephen cleaned my room.") She worked fast, raising a hum that provided a soothing background to my own work, punctuated by pacing cigarette breaks and mutters of outrage in her perfect WASP tones.

But in the fall we'd give up work in the afternoon, because fall is the time of the hunt. We'd go hawking, putting falcons into the sky fifty feet over brushy arroyos for desert quail, or a thousand feet above the oceanic sweep of the high plains south of Portales, where we made a once-a-year invited trip to chase prairie chickens. We'd run sighthounds, following on foot after jacks and covering hundreds of dirt-road miles perched in Floyd's orange dog truck in search of coyotes, a hunt I found nearly sinful but still incomparably stirring. We'd follow deer alone and with minimal kit in the wilderness foothills, or join the paramilitary food-gathering buck sweeps of the Torres family. I'd gasp and claw my way along impossible oak-clad side hills with John Davila in pursuit of elk, arms aching from the weight of a nine-pound black powder rifle, or crouch shaking in a blind on the Rio hoping a goose would have the bad luck to pass over and provide me with a hunter's Thanksgiving dinner.

We'd start the season with that social bird, the mourning dove. Betsy and I and Floyd and whichever of his sons was free from other duties would lurk in what seemed to be deadly ambush by a cattle watering tank, where the poor harassed birds would have to come and drink. And come they would, in twos and threes. We'd crouch, faces down, hearing their circling whistling wings; then stand, flaring them, and fire and fire, and miss and miss and miss, as they grabbed sky and twisted and dropped and turned and sped away. Betsy would often arm herself with a 35-MM Pentax and notebook to record the scene, and make the most accurate shots of us all.

But best were the last quail hunts of winter, because they combined the company of friends from far away, the bittersweet emotions of season's end, and those rare, still days of perfect weather that emerge from the frosts of winter. These were quests, expeditions; we'd discuss maps and populations and pack enormous picnics, all with the knowledge that in a couple of weeks there'd be no more hunting, only bills to be paid, friends scattered once more to the ends of the earth or at least the states, deadlines to be met, and waistlines that had been indulged all fall, trimmed by the easy discipline of the chase, to be reined in; in short, modern life.

First, this hunt, a trip of fifty miles on the dirt roads to the south, fourwheelers bumping through arroyo bottoms and lurching sideways over canyon rims. A change in vegetation occurs as you round the southern ramparts of the San Mateo range; the canyons become full of live oak and cottonwood as well as the ubiquitous juniper and cholla and prickly pear. On a south-facing slope something new appears: the bony whips of ocotillo.

The valley below seems as good as any. All the canyons hold populations of Gambel's quail, sleek little gray runners with markings of black and white and rust; this one has not been hunted by anyone this year. We release Tom's white setters, so much more delicate than our spaniels, and they begin to course in interlocking zigzags down the dry sand bed with its walls of spiky vegetation. Tom and his friend Laura follow immediately, with Floyd on the flank; Betsy and I hang back for a moment. Above, in a sky impossibly deep and cloudless, hang two golden eagles and a redtail, keeping precise spaces between them as they spiral up the same thermal.

We start down. Under the cottonwoods it smells like October in Vermont, and round leaves carpet the ground in the same way. I think I hear a lizard's rustle a little uphill, and ten-foot masts of yucca thrust up from their spiky collars on the canyon shoulders above. The dogs are on point, but shaky. A proper southwestern bushwhacker, I bustle up to run in. "Wait," pleads Tom. "They're not sure yet."

"They're running." This from Betsy, firmly. Floyd has already angled in from the side and as we converge ahead of the dogs we can hear the cackle of quail voices ahead of us. I speed up, clutching my gun, and the bushes erupt with forty or fifty little gray birds, calling, fluttering, and buzzing; some hesitating, some already halfway down the canyon; some going left, some hooking right, a few doubtless clinging to the security of the ground. Tom swings on one that is barely clearing the juniper, way over to my right; it drops a leg and curves down. He sends in his old dog. His young dog is already somewhere down the canyon, trying to fit his training to these barbaric running things that will not be held by his will.

The old dog finds the bird ten minutes later, dead, down a pack-rat hole. It is an animate flower, with a bobbing, sable comma over its beak as an almost ludicrous grace note. The young dog has returned, and all is forgiven. It is noon. We unpack the picnic hamper: fruit, sandwiches with cold venison and green chile jelly, cold breast of dove, dry, spiced sausage of venison and wild pig, and strong, red wine. I sit on the hood of Floyd's truck while the dogs pant in the shade. This afternoon my spaniels will have a chance to show their stuff. As we stretch and groan, momentarily reluctant to push on, a kestrel swings over the rim to hold, steady as a helicopter, above our heads. I point it out and Laura, grinning at the wonderful, ridiculous appropriateness of her choice, recites Gerard Manley Hopkins' "The Windhover" in its entirety. It may be the only time Hopkins has ever been applauded by a chorus of cowboy whoops and tossed Stetsons.

The year before I moved to Magdalena I read Jim Harrison's novella *Legends of the Fall*. One line in particular stuck in my memory: "Now he was to have seven years of grace, a period so relatively peerless and golden in his life that far into the future he would turn back to that time; the minutiae of the book of days, a hieratica relived slowly so that each page was turned with some eagerness." About six months after I read those words, Betsy Huntington and I drifted into Magdalena and began our own seven years of grace.

II

In the fall of 1979 I was back in Boston after spending a couple of years in a freezing back-road farmhouse in western Massachusetts. I was bored and broke, a perfect product of my time. I had left home at seventeen after four restless years on an undeserved scholarship at a Catholic prep school, after which I dropped incessantly in and out of college, grew my hair down my back, studied biology, worked in a lab, married, and divorced. I eventually began writing and sold the results; edited, lived in a converted chicken coop with falcons and dogs, and roamed up and down the country in search of God only knew what. Twelve years later I had a fair if somewhat obscure reputation as a freelance writer. I was a naturalist without credentials who lived to hunt and read. I wanted to be Teddy Roosevelt, Will Beebe, Richard Meinertzhagen, Denys Finch-Hatton, or, more modestly, Gavin Maxwell or Peter Matthiessen. I had expensive tastes in belongings, adventure, and alchohol. (I can hear Bets: "Didn't you ever realize that all those people are richer than God?") I had two fifty-year-old L. C. Smith sidelock shotguns, one engraved, five hundred books, a master-falconer's license, and a captive-bred lanner falcon with ancestors from South Africa and Ethiopia. I liked my life, but had nobody to talk to.

We had been out flying hawks. My ne'er-do-well friend Michael (a Yalie who had taken to waiting tables, commercial fishing, and professional drinking), his ferocious sometime girlfriend Shelagh, and I were having shots and beers in a falconer's kitchen in central Massachusetts when I remembered that I was supposed to be at a party at Annie's.

"That zoo woman? She's great, let's go!"

Less than moved by Michael's reflexive lechery, Shelagh held back. I had to call, anyway. "Bring Michael too," said Annie. "There's somebody here I'd like you to meet."

It was almost an hour's drive. We started singing fifties rock 'n' roll songs, serious doo-wop stuff: "Blue Moon," "Get a Job," "Little Star," "Silhouettes." Michael and I worked ourselves up to such pitch of hilarity as we harmonized and soothed our throats with beer that Shelagh asked to be let out. By the time we entered the heat, light, and clutter of Annie's basement I was goofy, as much from song as from drink. Annie hugged me and asked me how my bird was doing.

That question will always sober up a falconer. "Annie, can I put him in the back room? I don't like to leave him in Michael's van." As Annie was indeed "that zoo woman" she didn't find the request odd. She went to prepare a perch and some newspaper for the floor. I returned in a moment with the hooded lanner falcon and sideslipped through the crowd, bird hand hugged in close under my left shoulder as I led with my right hand. I didn't think a single one of the noisy partygoers had so much as seen the bird.

When I turned from getting a real drink, a short, athletic

woman was standing in front of me. She had a helmet of straight gray-blond hair, cut in bangs at eyebrow level but coming down nearly to her shoulders on the sides, and wore a blue-and-white, horizontally striped sailor's jersey. Despite her trim figure, I could see that she was the oldest person in the room.

"You're the 'falconer and writer' " (I could see the quotes). "I'm the 'woman with the cats who writes.' Give me a Camel." Her drawled patrician vowels were incongruous in the setting. She didn't smile immediately, but squinted at me sideways as I lit her cigarette. "I gave these up months ago. God, they taste good. Tell me about the bird."

If I ever stop drinking it will be because of lost memories. But we lose them anyway; how can we know, at the times that precede conscious decision, that we are at some point in which every word and gesture must change our lives irrevocably? I remember that she told me of sailing rented boats in Boston Harbor. "I'm a jock," she said proudly, showing me the muscle tone in her slender arm. I remember telling her that the record that was playing, Warren Zevon's *Bad Luck Streak in Dancing School*, was dedicated to *"il miglior fabbro,"* the mystery writer Ross MacDonald. She looked blank. "You know, Eliot to Pound. *The Waste Land.*"

She grinned suddenly, dazzlingly. Betsy's grin, teeth gleaming from ear to ear, eyes crinkled shut, could illuminate a room. "Nobody in your generation reads Eliot."

"Now you know two who do: me 'n Warren Zevon."

We didn't talk to anybody else all night. We smoked all the Camels, drank ourselves cold sober, talked about breeding wildcats, bobcat habits, hunting and falconry and literature both high and low, of the Beatles, and, I swear, Cole Porter. Somehow, sometime in the morning, we got onto the prose of World War I poets. She was reading Sassoon, *Memoirs of a Fox Hunting Man*; I was going through *Goodbye to All That* for the second time. We were interrupted by Annie's loud "Enough!"

We looked over. She was stretched out on the couch, looking rumpled. The apartment was empty, except for a hundred beer cans, a thousand butts.

"You people can do what you want. But as far as I'm concerned, Sassoon is a fucking hairdresser, and I'm going to bed."

I walked Betsy to the car. The sun was up. I hugged her impulsively, and asked her if she would meet me for lunch the next day. Later, much later, she would confess to me: "I figured the kid had a lot of nerve. But he talked a good line, so what the heck?"

I was to see Michael that afternoon. Over beers at the gin mill in Inman Square, he spoke of the party. "That blonde zoo girl's husband almost punched me. The only interesting woman there was that older one you were talking to. Do you have her name? I think I'll ask her out."

"The hell you will. I already have."

Our second "date" was at a Szechwan restaurant. As she entered I had a stab of doubt. She had cut her hair extremely short and was wearing her working clothes, a tweed suit; she looked older, and formidable. What was I doing there? But the unease retreated into the background as we began to talk again. I was wary of much more than our differences in age. I knew that Annie had wanted us to meet. To say that I distrust matchmaking is only to admit that I occasionally show flashes of sanity. All Betsy knew of me, she later said, was that I trained falcons and "wrote," which in our time can, and usually does mean almost any kind of dilettantism or posing. And what I knew about her was that she was older than I and also "wrote." I was, perhaps still am, the kind of anti-snob who is, of course, a ferocious snob, and had been convinced that with her accent and name she was likely to be a wealthy lightweight who played at writing and animal keeping.

She was none of the above. She had, at times, been richer than I could imagine, but she was now a low-salary journalist for MIT's newspaper. Her animal-keeping was serious; she had been the first person to breed the Central American margay cat in captivity. And far from being a trust-fund baby from a Boston Brahmin family, Elizabeth Catharine Huntington had been born in backwoods China, youngest daughter of an ancient Anglican bishop who had been there from 1892 until 1939. Betsy (she renamed herself at twelve after the adventurous heroine of a favorite book) was separated in age from her siblings by a fair gap. When she was born her father was sixty-three, her mother forty-five. She claimed, "When I was born we converted the village; if I had been male we would have converted the province." Her mother, as most colonial mothers of her class in eastern countries did, left her upbringing to her amah; I have more than one photo of Betsy with the nurse, whom she loved, and not one with her mother Virginia until, at eight, she appears with her atop a camel, with the Great Pyramid in the background.

Betsy spoke Chinese before English, ate first with chopsticks ("Mother's idea of food was boiled oatmeal and canned salmon," she would say with distaste) and kept strange pets. Her sister Jane recalls that when Betsy was very young, she would do what she was not supposed to, spank herself, and go to the corner. At twelve, at one of the bewildering successions of schools that ranged from Dana Hall to a farm in New Hampshire, she broke her two upper incisors in the first of a lifelong succession of horse accidents. She went to Wellesley and lasted a semester. At twenty-one she came into an inheritance and embarked on several years of improbable adventure. In a memoir written years later, big-game guide and rare-gun dealer Mike Evans said that "Betsy had quite a sum of money at one time and had traveled it all away. I guess she didn't want to wake up one day to find that money had her by the leg." She bought a Mercedes and drove at furious speeds through the Pyrenees, took at least one driving lesson from Juan Fangio, helped a boyfriend (who died without paying back the loan) buy an island in the Caribbean, and met a parade of dazzling and dubious characters, most of whom will forever remain anonymous. And when, the lotus-eating years done, she found herself penniless, she put herself through Boston University and got a journalism degree. Through the rest of her life, except during her marriage to a brilliant but violent and unstable inventor (he drove a racing car into a tree several years after they split) she supported herself as a journalist, copywriter, and literary jack-of-all-trades.

Our absolute ease and ability to complete each other's sentences must have disarmed everyone, from my crusty father to Betsy's splendidly odd family to the ranchers of the back-country west; we were accepted everywhere. I needed that. I was absolutely happy when I was with her, but, to my disgust, conventional enough to be uneasy about our differences. After eight years I suppose we changed and became more like one another, but, especially at first, we must have seemed an odd couple. She was twenty years older, her accents formed at Dana Hall and

Chatham Hall, accents that she denied existed. "I sound just like your family," she'd insist, "except now I'm picking up a western accent." She never did. In fact, six years after we had moved to Magdalena, she heard herself for the first time on a tape and was appalled. "My God, Stephen," she said, "I sound like a lady from Philadelphia!"

I am descended on my father's side from Alpine Italian peasants, on my mother's from Canadian Maritimes "herring chokers," tidewater potato farmers, Irish tavern owners, and Bavarian burghers, Roman Catholic to a man and woman. My parents are almost-normal suburbanites. My father owns his own small engineering company, and my mother paints. But there is a hint of romance for those who look closer—my father once had a scholarship to the Museum School of Fine Arts, my mother an art degree, and they met as students. After World War II, during which my father flew B-17's over Germany—on my wall is a harrowing ink drawing, done between missions, of fighters rising to meet the bombers, a B-17 curving down in flames—he returned home with an enormous English pointer from Texas, a 16-cylinder Cadillac roadster, and ambitions. My grandfather, a hard man who worked in granite quarries all his life, banished the car ("You're not gonna park no rich man's car here"). And soon after, my father switched from art to civil engineering. Despite his success, he had all the distrust of WASPs inherent in a Boston ethnic's background; his favorite term for those of Betsy's background was "inbred overbites."

One afternoon, under the pressure of some inarticulate obligation, we made a running visit to my parents' home. My mother hovered uneasily; far from being put off by Betsy's background, I think she was impressed by it, but also a little intimidated. Perhaps projecting her own worries, though, she managed to whisper to me that my father ("He's so old-fashioned!") might disapprove of our age difference. We were nervous too, and soon found an excuse to leave. As I warmed up the car I heard a knock on the window. My father had driven up and sized up the situation. He leaned in and grinned. "What's the hurry? Ashamed of your old man?" We went back in for a shot of whiskey. Soon, to my amazement and near jealousy, they were laughing together like lifelong friends.

Betsy's mother Virginia posed a different problem, at least for me; I was terrified by her. She was a self-created grande-dame, the granddaughter of a German Mennonite from Illinois, who had converted to the Anglican church, gone to China, and married the bishop. She combined a real but half-ironic snobbery, with aggressively democratic opinions. ("She would have gone all the way to Rome," Bets would mutter, "except that it wasn't chic!") During the war she was appalled when Packard suspended production—since she replaced them every year, she thought they wore out every year. Postwar economics led her to buy and drive her own Fords, one of which she rejected because "above eighty it wiggles." After her husband's death she occupied her time writing bad poetry and commuting to Mexico for the winter.

All of these stories, and worse, combined to scare me. I was told not to worry, that Virginia loved men, despite treating her daughters as difficult teenagers. Betsy's sixty-eight-year-old sister Jane told me that "I don't think of her as Mother; it's easier to get along with her if I think of her as an interesting character that I know." Betsy's response was to quote a poem that Virginia had written to her on her fourth birthday, "To Beth at Four:"

I will give you heaven's keys
So Beth sings, old melodies.
Ah, my darling future tense
Is past and present too, the sense
Is wedded firm in happy fact,
Lacking you, 'twas heaven we lacked.
Unto us a gift is given.
You yourself are keys of heaven.

"Then," she added, "she sent me away to school and I didn't see her again 'til I was fourteen."

When I met her she was ninety-four. She held court in a plush retirement home in Concord, full of old China hands and ancient Unitarians, a tiny woman with downy-white hair, a strong jaw, and the coke-bottle glasses of a cataract victim. When we were introduced she pulled my head down and asked me how many brothers and sisters I had.

"Eight. I'm the oldest of nine."

She turned to Betsy, still holding on to my ears. "Ah. Roman Catholic, I see." But by the time I left she was asking me to come and read my writing to her, and accusing me of trying to kiss her. I felt I could at least breathe in her presence.

For the first time in either of our lives, we each had someone whom we could talk to about everything. In our case this included falcons and margay cats, Evelyn Waugh and P. G. Wodehouse, Kingsley Amis, Dorothy Sayers and John D. MacDonald, her beloved Sitwells and my Karen Blixen, shotguns and horses, Mozart and the Clash, the Beatles and Cole Porter, Montana and Paris, four-wheel-drive vehicles and old Mercedes roadsters. She told me of dirt roads in the Pyrenees and Mexico, of seeing Noel Coward, stark naked, play the piano at a party in Jamaica, while her very Catholic friend Joan murmured that it was charming, but he might have paused to put on a bathing suit. She remembered her brother's camping trip in China with the Boy Scouts, when each scout had a personal servant to carry his pack, build fires, and make his bedroll, and a runner was sent back to town every day for mail. "Jon did get to carry the flag . . ." She would quote Jane Austen to my Hemingway and T. H. White. We both had good books by Gavin Maxwell, Anthony Burgess and both Durrell brothers. Our lives, like our record collections, libraries and cars (her unexpected silver Trans-Am, my Toyota jeep) dovetailed, fit together in a complicated joint of curves and angles like the wood and metal of one of my ancient handmade double guns. I began to realize with amazement that I had a partner in love and crime, another person who could truly say that she did, within the limits that the world imposed, exactly what she desired. We had made our pact to live together for the rest of our lives, long before we acknowledged it in words.

There is a phrase my friends use today: "alone," or "so alone." It means being so far off in your own world that you are incomprehensible to anyone else. And it strikes me now that without our being in any way antisocial, we became "alone" together very fast. We never explained anything or tried to make plans, at least in those days. My life had taught me to live from day to day. It was all stories we could tell. She'd entertain me with tales of her family, how her two sisters founded a Trotskyite commune on Beacon Hill in the forties, and how the police, entering one night, found various boys and girls together and charged them with "lewd and lascivious cohabitation." Fierce Mary ("She was in it to throw bombs," claimed Bets) was indignant when her friend Kim gallantly offered, in front of the judge, to marry her—she was a woman, or rather a young girl, of principles, one of which was then still called "free love." The matter was eventually resolved to everyone's relief, but not before the neighbors testified that the house was obviously one of ill repute. Every week an old lady would be chauffeured to the door by a large black man driving a Packard. Who else could she be but the madam? Whether Virginia or her Haitian chauffeur Herve was more embarrassed is not recorded.

She entered my world, too, becoming a regular at the Inn Square bar where I spent my evenings and had once worked. One night a fight broke out and as I moved to shield her I saw her firmly clutching a long-neck bottle by its neck. After the bouncers had evicted the troublemakers I asked her what the hell she thought she was doing. She was hurt. "I didn't see anybody else moving to back you up." I took her grouse hunting for the first time and, improbably, killed the first bird I fired at, giving her a forever-prejudiced idea of my shooting ability. We flew the lanner on a local baseball diamond, and brought Betsy's business talents to bear picking up secondhand guns.

I had moved into her apartment on the first floor of a building in Newton, Massachusetts, more or less without planning to. It was as easy as that, as though it were part of a plan already laid, one neither of us ever questioned or kicked back against; sure, comfortable, and merry. I tried, perhaps a month in, to explain to her what I thought was happening: that, above even romance, I had been convinced from our first half-hour's conversation that she was my best possible friend, forever and ever; that I wanted this conversation to go on and on; that if I let anything—convention, our friends, or either of our families—get in the way, it would be our greatest loss. "Yes," she said, "Hush, lamb," and fell asleep. Her ability to sleep anywhere and anytime, against my perpetual insomnia, was just another of our unimportant differences.

Newton was a real suburb. A neighbor saw Betsy carrying in her saddle one day, dressed in boots and riding pants. He asked her if she rode horseback. His kids saw us with our duck guns one morning and fled screaming, convinced, he later told us, that we were terrorists. We took him and the kids fishing. He told us later he now understood fishing: it was like sex, or teaching a good class. We bought an enormous springer spaniel with a rock-hard head, and almost lost him when he followed the mailman. Another neighbor watched us fly the lanner and told his daughter it was a model airplane.

One night we were relaxing with drinks after dinner at the house of some good, very civilized friends, watching a PBS nature film. The usual cheetah began the usual slow-motion chase after the usual gazelle. The music swelled to a crescendo then stopped dead as the action blurred into real-life speed, dust, and stillness. Betsy and I raised our glasses and clinked them. Our hostess had left the room and her husband looked at us, puzzled. "You know," he said, "You're the only people I've ever seen who cheer the bad guys in the animal shows."

I had always nursed a half-rational, half-romantic fascination with the Rocky Mountain west, fed equally by hunting magazines, falconers' tales, an extended trip in 1971, and the writings of various contemporary exurbanites. Both of us had lived in primitive conditions, coped with outhouses and animal husbandry and oil lamps, as well as city apartments. On the whole, we were beginning to think that we liked the first set of problems better. Betsy had wandered through Europe and Mexico, but had never been on the ground west of the Mississippi. I began to correspond with a writer in darkest New Mexico who had sent me one of his essays. M. H. Salmon bred sighthounds, salukis, greyhounds, and Scottish deerhounds, ran them at coyotes and hares, took wonderful photos, and wrote with wit and style. He invited us to visit.

"Wanna move out west?"

"I don't know. We could wait a couple of years. I could retire early from MIT, and we'd have a pension."

"Marry me?"

She looked shocked. "Good God, no! I'm much too antique for you. You need to marry a young woman, someone who can have children."

"Only after you die."

"Thank you, lamb. Ask me again in six months. But maybe we should move. Maybe we can even find a cheap horse."

Our friends had mixed emotions about the idea. Betsy's oldest crony, in New York, worried about what the arid atmosphere of the west would do to her complexion. "Besides," she said to Bets, "Didn't you once tell me that you would never go more than twenty feet off the pavement?" Others thought we were insane. We weren't, just restless. We bought a capped Datsun king-cab pickup in pitted yellow. With less than 20,000 miles on the odometer it was already etched by New England's salty winters. Our friend Cooper fitted the bed with a box which acted as both sleeping platform and storage. We filled the space below with novels and poetry and bird guides, fishing rods, cooking utensils, a 20-gauge sliding-breech Darne shotgun from France and a 28-gauge AyA from Spain. We bought a tape deck for the cab and loaded up on tapes of road music: Zevon, Hank Williams, Mozart horn concertos by Dennis Brain, Vivaldi, Fred Neill. We sold Betsy's car and my crumbling Toyota Land Cruiser and left Newton, hungover but full of anticipation on a dark January morning. We were wearing the official trip T-shirts our friends had given us the night before. On the front they said "Truth or Consequences" and on the back, "Don't take me alive."

III

We reached New Mexico in March, up through El Paso on a day so clear and cold it looked like you could see all the way north to the Sangre de Cristos on the Colorado border. We had been traveling through the bleak mountains and Chihuhuan desert scrub of West Texas for two days, as true a western landscape as you can find. North of there, the first ramparts of the Gila Country, the ten-thousand-foot-plus castellations of the Black Range, began to rise up on our left, miles and miles away across creosote-bush flats. They were alpine and toothy and looked as though they had glaciers on top—real mountains. Across the river on our right, so far away we had no idea of the scale, were more and different ridges, rosy dinosaurian backbones, low, desert, barren. When we saw an eagle turn over the empty road we stopped in a kind of ecstasy and got out to stand on the roadside to breathe and turn in circles and wave our arms. What was this place?

Much later we were flying falcons on the endless grassy mesa west of Albuquerque. By then we were used to seeing things like the Sandias, the "Watermelon Mountains" that rose like a breaking wave four thousand feet above the Rio flats twenty miles east of us, ribboned with rock strata that I supposed could have resembled sliced melons to a fanciful early settler and given them their name. Betsy, looking south past a symmetrical volcanic cone, saw a familiar blue ridge. "Those look like the Magdalenas—there, to the right of Ladron Peak."

"They are."

"But they're seventy miles away."

Everybody looked at her. After a moment she added, "We're from the east. You can't see seventy miles in the east."

Annette Slifka, born and raised in Idaho, looked at her in amazement. "What gets in the way?"

We stayed that night in Socorro, which was to become "town," as in Tom McGuane's memorable piece of mistrust for the settled: "town is for supplies." We stayed in a motel that allowed dogs, ate green chile, and woke in the morning to meadowlarks' sweet whistles in the vacant lot beside us. Walking Spud, I looked up past the igneous monolith of "M Mountain" to more mountains, not visibly higher but with the Pleistocene air and blue snow fields of the Black Range farther south. It was my first close-up look at foothills, mountains behind. A puzzled flatlander, I had no idea but that I wanted to be up there.

As far as I could see, the nearest motel to Dutch Salmon's High Lonesome was in Socorro. He had drawn a careful map showing a drive of untotalled miles west, through villages called Magdalena and Datil and Pie Town. Well past the last, a dirt road was marked heading due south past signposts reading "old adobe church" and "cattle guard," ending in a circle labeled "three miles on left fork, see mobile home on left; that's it," with the added legend, "It's not as tough as it looks."

We tried to call. The operator informed us that the phones were out west of Datil. Since we had the map and boundless ignorance, we just drove on out.

Or up. West of Socorro the road makes a long straight run up a sort of gentle ramp, through the beginnings of grass and the last few hardy clumps of creosote. About five miles out we could see a wall of gnarly black rock that seemed to stand across our path. Soon we could not ignore the closing walls. The road cut into them. Now the road began to lean left, then right. A vertical-walled canyon yawned on the left, disappeared; we zigzagged again and emerged into a series of long switchbacks around immense grassy shoulders, going up and up and up and up. We could see segments of road cutting left and right far above, always with those peaks behind.

We toiled up, shifted down to third, pulled over to let a roaring pickup pass. It had a bumper sticker that said, "Navajo Goat Ropers Make Better Lovers."

And up, and up, shifting to second. In the brilliant but deep-shadowed morning light Betsy was reminded of Scotland, something about treeless hills and cows grazing in the distance, dark scrub, cold air. It was out of my experience, and my thoughts roamed somewhere between "this sure isn't Kansas," *et in arcadia ego*, and even a little bit of dizzy fear.

Then we topped out, on a grass plain as flat and nappy as a brown-felt pool table. The road ran northwest, straight as if ruled. I pulled the truck over. To the left, parallel to the road, blue foothills and white peaks, another level—actually two, but my mind could not yet sort out mountain landscape—the Magdalenas. To the right, plains to the limit of vision, one perfectly symmetrical volcano in the middle distance, and a line of peculiar grassy hills like frozen breakers edging the plateau's rim. Behind us, a steep fall of road, the Rio, desert peaks beyond. The only human artifacts included the road, a wire fence, and a power line. Three ravens made away, muttering, from a roadside trash can.

Betsy's response was awe: "Oh, my." Mine was sudden, odd

familiarity. Ahead and to the right, the shape of the land resembled my dim memories of Montana's front range country. And my God but it looked big.

The road's next segment took us northward on a gentle incline, past a solitary bar—the only building on the pavement between Socorro and Magdalena—and on over a plain until the northern nose of the Magdalenas plunged into the ground. The road curved blindly left around that shoulder. To our right, to the north, we could see a few bare hills with a far-off line of white-capped mountains behind. We didn't know it that first time, but the highest point there was Mount Taylor, over a hundred miles away.

The hills dropped back. To the south we could see for miles into a bay in the mountains. Hanging over the oncoming village was a bare ridge topped by a cliff, Magdalena Mountain itself, an isolated hogback that looked like a different species from the more distant peaks. We were to see this sight on awakening for the next seven years, but right now, other than to make conventional sounds of admiration for the shape of the southern horizon, we never slowed down. A little farther on Magdalena's adobes and turn-of-the-century business buildings lined up beside a half-mile of narrow highway. We saw three bars, the Golden Spur, Paris Tavern, and West Bar, five gas stations, and one market, the Trail's End. The cross streets all ended in a couple of blocks; only two were paved.

Then, out of town, past windmills and increasing junipers, piñon pines, and cows. The landscape kept stretching, getting bigger and bigger, as the road climbed over hills that looked gentle but required us to shift down every time. Patches of snow began to accumulate beneath the pines, and the fences were full of glowing, turquoise, mountain bluebirds, fluttering and whirling like animated bits of New Mexican sky.

From the top of the last hill a flat, blue surface filled the entire space below until it stopped on a ruled horizon to the south. It looked like the sea. We were puzzled until we drove out of the last piñon-clad waves and onto its surface. Close up the surface lost its blue and changed to the brown of dead grass. The road stretched due west like a diagram of perspective, utterly flat and straight and triangular, a pointer to a distant cluster of blue-hill cutouts. South was nothing but horizon. And across our path was a scattering of man-made white objects that didn't scan at all. Stonehenge? Golf tees of the gods?

The Plain of San Augustine was marked on our road map, if not Dutch Salmon's homemade job; the white objects increased in size for fifteen minutes and turned into an array of hundred-foot, chalk-white radio telescopes, their faces aligned like cloned mechanical flowers. The line stretched across our path on rubber-insulated railroad tracks, as beautiful as a sculpture or a formal garden on the geometric surface of the plain.

Beneath them were black bricks that resolved into cows, brangus and black angus; white dots, clustered, the markings on a ghostly herd of antelope; shining white ferruginous hawks with rust leggings, capping fenceposts; and more black ravens, flying with purpose. Other than the very large array, the only signs of humans were windmills, a solitary ranch house well back from the road, and a cattle tank with a large sign that said "Solar Water Heater."

When the highway reentered the waiting hills thirty miles on, the landscape became normal Rocky Mountain. We had been climbing steadily if imperceptibly all the way, and were now above seven thousand feet. From there to Mangas the road led through canyons and around mesas, mostly with pine trees and eroded rock and patches of snow in sight. We crossed the Continental Divide at Pie Town, smallest living town between Socorro and Springerville, in Arizona. Ten miles farther west in the middle of absolutely nowhere, a hand-lettered sign pointed south down a dirt and mud track, over ten more miles of dry rabbit brush to more blue mountains: "Mangus."

Our arrival at High Lonesome—a trailer house, to use the proper terminology, in a broad flat surrounded by piñon-juniper arms, two miles from the nearest neighbor, twelve miles from any pavement—was anticlimactic. We churned through a last quarter-mile of mud-rut driveway to find nobody home but an amazing pack of dogs: salukis with silken coats and huge eyes, scarred brindle greyhounds with graying muzzles, an immense Scottish deerhound with a low-hung head, like a hairy dinosaur, blueticks, a Plott, red dogs with hound voices and airedale whiskers, and a weird low-slung spotted beast, all howling and baying and standing on the truck. When I rolled down the window, three climbed over each other to lick my hand. Encouraged, I braved the pack to leave a note stuck on the trailer door (something on the lines of "We're here—Bonanza Motel in Socorro—call") turned around, and drove the 110-odd miles back, to almost immediately pick up the phone and hear, "Come on out."

We were a mix of curious and just a little worried about Dutch. Would he like us? After all, we knew no westerners, and we were real Eastern. Even as I write that, "real Eastern," I realize it's a western locution, and I am, if Eastern, now more than a bit Western as well. Meanwhile, Dutch and his then girlfriend were knee-deep in apprehension about meeting us. Dutch had worked himself up into a state of believing that I would show up wearing a Brooks Brothers suit. I think he had also spoken to Betsy, whose accent might well have added to his apprehension.

We bumped in again. The same wave of dogs rolled over our truck. I waded through them to the corral behind the trailer. Unsaddling a scruffy black horse was the most ancient and decrepit cowboy I have ever seen, in or out of a western movie. He had a hat crusted with overlapping sweat stains, three-days' beard, six-months' grime, and no teeth. He swayed toward me, hand extended, gargling something incomprehensible, stopped, and turned to pick an open can of beer off a fence post. As I stood petrified, hand firmly extended, I heard a voice behind me.

"Mr. Bodio? M. H. Salmon here." I turned and saw a man of about my own age emerging from the trailer. He looked like a cowboy in a Charles Russell painting rather than one on television—aged fedora instead of a ten-gallon hat, red bandanna, flannel shirt, chaps—and wore dark glasses and a blond moustache. As I shook my new friend's hand, I didn't know that his relief at seeing a figure in boots and red L. L. Bean chamois shirt was as great as mine in seeing him. He introduced me to "Rex"—more gibberish, a wave of the beer can—and I introduced him to Betsy. In the trailer, his girlfriend said they were afraid we would be carrying briefcases.

On our way back to Socorro we saw a "For Rent" sign on a little house fifty feet north of the road, a mile east of town. Across the street to the south stood Magdalena's most prominent landmark, still imposing today with its roof burnt off—an immense Victorian brick house with anachronistic pillars that commands the eastern approach to town like a guard post. People from Connecticut whom you meet at parties and who have driven once along Route 60 to Phoenix remember that house, but not the one directly across the street—a low, rectangular, flat-topped structure that resembled a blue brick. Two fine Siberian elms shaded the front walk, and a picket fence surrounded the yard. Its address, we would find, was simply "Route 60, East of Magdalena."

We stopped on impulse to look. We couldn't see much through the windows, and the car wedged between the door and the fence did not inspire confidence. Still, the house was an attractive distance from town. We were only two hours from Albuquerque, and the rent couldn't be too high. "Let's try it for the summer," suggested Betsy. We still had to go to Nevada and California (as a favor to Dutch we had agreed to deliver a greyhound to Sacramento) but maybe the landlord would hold it for a month.

We called the number. After some confusion about identity on both ends, we found that our plan would suit our new landlady, who wanted a month to get the place ready. We paid the deposit and drove into the sunset, past the Sierras to where the suburbs began again. We spent the month eating and partying in San Francisco, delivering the greyhound to Sacramento, and searching for falcon nests in the Shoshone Range near Battle Mountain, Nevada. It was April when we returned, intending to stay for a couple of months.

They were huddled over a pit in the backyard when we came around the house: our landlady, a thin man in black with a style straight out of my fifties youth, and an old woman improbably dressed in a print dress, running shoes, and poke bonnet. The hole looked like a septic tank but was dry. A stack of railroad ties stood by the edge. The landlady looked embarrassed. "These are the people who are going to rent the house," she announced to the air.

The man in black turned to her as though she had just proposed something ridiculous. "We can't leave this hole for these people."

Betsy and I felt uncomfortable, as though we had interrupted a family argument. We excused ourselves and drifted around to the front to look at the dead car. I had lived in more than one rural backwater, and all real backwaters have "yard cars"—dead vehicles kept around out of prudence or laziness, parked, according to the industry of the owners, on blocks or deflated tires. But this was an exceptional specimen. It was a Mercury Comet of about 1962 vintage. It had no wheels and no interior; in fact, when we looked through the windows we saw that it had no chassis or floorboards, only sand and dead weeds. It was wedged, lengthwise, tightly, between the picket fence and one of the two front doors. On its sandblasted side was stenciled the word "comet" in foot-high Gothic letters.

The landlady came around the corner. "I'll get rid of that car for you."

"Thanks."

"Though you might want to keep it. You could use it for a dog bed." Maybe she interpreted my speechless silence as agreement, for you could feel her warming to the idea. "You could keep your cat in there, too. You could put a bed for it up under the back window. Blankets in the bottom." I think she sensed that I didn't think it a great idea, because she trailed off, "Mama kept chickens in it . . ." and briskly changed the subject. "Let me show you inside."

The inside was clean and whitewashed, if oddly broken up. I didn't count the rooms at the time but there were thirteen, all small and utterly asymmetrical. Four were obviously bedrooms. One, containing the oil burner, was an uneasy compromise between a closet and a room, with both a door and a half door at opposite ends. One had a raised linoleum floor and a boarded-up door (all the others were carpeted). And one, reached through the bathroom, was an enormous enclosed porch with modern sliding windows on the outside north walls and four more permanently shut glass windows leading into the kitchen. The porch was full of junk, including a television sans picture tube ("You could put plants in this") and a refrigerator box filled to the brim with empty bleach bottles. But the rest was clean, empty, and apparently functioning, not to mention huge.

After our tour of the house, the landlady insisted on showing us around town to smooth our transition. She took us to the town hall to start our water and water bill ("He's a writer, he's gonna write about this town, just like Zane Gray"); to the house of a little old lady who said she had "stories" but who refused to speak to us because she had been "misquoted"; and finally, to meet the postmaster, a dapper man with a neat goatee and a grave hidalgo's manner.

When we returned to the house the man in black ("My son . . . I don't know what got into him. He thought he buried something down there, but he can't remember what") was gone, the hole had vanished, and the old woman in the bonnet was standing by her truck. "I can't believe you painted the trim that color," she proclaimed. "It's so ugly."

"I think it's fine, mama. What do you people think?" It was ugly, a sort of mustard yellow. But we were seized with an overwhelming desire to be alone with the house, mixed with misgivings about the whole enterprise, and managed to see them off, with promises of a new stove within the next couple of days.

The first time we awakened to the mountains, the sun rose from over the shoulder of the Magdalenas to illuminate the landscape with chilly precision. The peaks loomed over the world from across the street, simultaneously near and remote, blue-treed, white-snowed. The brush in the foreground was pale gold, the meadowlark singing atop a cholla an impossible yellow. I went out to walk the dogs. After the night's loud wind the air was still. Sleepy, ill-rested, I was still full of the conviction that I would come to love the landscape. I was a little apprehensive about the people. Buried something?

After coffee I attacked the yard. The cleanup had not extended to the fenced half-acre around the house. There were enough silvery-gray boards there, half-hidden by four-foot weeds, to build another house. I submerged my misgivings in sweat, and commenced to stack wood. I had finished two waist-high piles, mostly of one-by-twelve planks, when a pickup swerved off the road and pulled up to stop in front of our door, engine running.

Urban people, insulated by staircases and door buzzers, come to your door; westerners, we were to find, will more often than not wait in the car. When no one emerged I put down my plank and walked over. A handsome, dark-haired woman in her forties got out.

"I'm Shirley Tarpley and this is my boyfriend Tommy Torres.

You can call him Chubby." She was Anglo and pale and spoke with a ranch accent; the man behind the wheel was short and broad, with the copper-brown skin of Mexican-Indian descent, high cheekbones, sideburns, and a great, drooping, black moustache. She wore jeans and boots and a western shirt; he a sleeveless T-shirt and a tractor cap. He grinned and spat tobacco juice into a coffee can he held in his right hand.

Years have brought me the patience not to jump into western conversations; I didn't have it then. "Yes?"

"Matt down at the post office sent us. We do odd jobs or almost anything. He thought you could use a little yard work."

I certainly could. I needed to sit down and do some quick-bucks writing, immediately. But I had never in my life hired anybody to do anything, never mind something I could do myself. I felt self-conscious in this new role; also, did these people think we were rich easterners, able to pay vast sums of money?

"Uh, I don't know. I mean, I could use a little help. But we're pretty broke."

"That's all right. We don't ask for much."

Somehow I found myself agreeing, as much because I didn't know how to say no as for any other reason. They agreed to come back in a few hours and I went in, bemused, to inform Betsy of my decision.

I was eating lunch when I heard a grate of metal on metal and looked out to see Chubby stroking the blade of his hoe with a metal file. I quelled my conscience—or gave in to my shyness— and dragged out a stack of yellow legal pads. Best to occupy myself in trying to make some money, if there were going to be people working for me. Betsy, always easier with strangers, went out to talk. She had gone for errands and returned with the information that a local woman, another introduction from Matt at the post office, had recommended wages of ten dollars a day. We both agreed that was ridiculous, but how much was right?

Two hours later all the tall weeds were uprooted and piled in mounds. I went out with three beers. Chubby looked surprised, then nodded. He hadn't yet said a word.

"How much do you want for this?"

"Oh, whatever. Ask Shirley."

I looked at Shirley. "I don't know. We just started doing this. Whatever you think is fair."

"Well, I don't know either. I never hired anybody." At this point we were all grinning in helpless embarrassment. "How about . . . does fifty dollars sound right?"

"That's too much!" from Chubby crossed "We only got twenty for a day-and-a-half last week!" from Shirley. I was relieved but still confused.

"How about thirty? You could help me take the stuff on the porch to the dump."

"Sounds good to me." This from Chubby, firmly. His hand was extended. I shook it, and, though I could not know it, began living in Magdalena.

The phone that I had seen never turned up. Bets kept asking me if I was sure I had seen one. I'd begun to doubt my sanity, for I had a perfect memory of it: yellow, behind the right-hand front door. Then we ran into the landlady in the Socorro supermarket. I browsed ahead as she and Betsy spoke. Betsy came back giggling and with her perfect ear for accents intoned, "I'm so ashamed. Mama stole your phone. I didn't see it 'til I was halfway home. I said, 'Mama, you can't steal those people's phone.' "

"Great. Is she bringing it back?"

"This afternoon. With some rugs. And the stove."

I was in the back porch, trying to pull nails out of the firmly attached door so that I could remove some of the accumulated objects, when the landlady arrived. I emerged through the bathroom to see the dry corpse of a rat fall out of the bottom of the gas stove that she was carrying single-handedly. She didn't miss a step. "Baby rat," she grunted, kicking it aside.

In a minute she had the stove hooked up. "Come on out and see if you want these rugs." All three were rolled and tied and encrusted with dust and white feathers. I grabbed one and dragged it out of the truck bed. She threw the other over the side, untied the string on one, and began to unroll it: a purple triangle about ten feet on a side. Mine was a more conventional burnt orange and appeared to be a rectangle. "You're gonna have to hose these down some. Just spread 'em out here in the yard and wash this stuff off and let 'em dry for a few days and they'll be good as new."

"What's on them?" I knew what it looked like.

"Oh, I had them stored in the chicken coop for the last couple of years. They got a few bird specks."

Chubby and Shirley soon became my first window into New Mexico, though Chubby could puzzle me. He told me of a couple who had their votes bought by the party chairman in a local city, with a check credited on its face to the same party. I must have looked thunderstruck, not morally—after all, I'd come from Boston—but at the openness of it. Shirley hastened to reassure me. "Don't worry. They didn't vote; they spent it on a dentist." Next it was the idea of an "Anglo." Both Chubby and Shirley insisted that Betsy and I were Anglos. No one of even partial Italian descent in Boston could consider himself Anglo, but Chubby insisted. "Italians are Anglos." He brought up Senator Pete Domenici ("Domeneechi"), whose style is as Ivy League as that of George Bush, but then overplayed his hand by insisting that the Chinese, Venezuelan-born, Spanish-speaking acupuncturist in Socorro was also an Anglo.

There was also the matter of accent and vocabulary. I soon learned that if Chubby used a trisyllabic word that he was likely to be using it correctly, however odd the context. When he told me his uncle was building "an atrocity" in the yard, the sight that greeted me when I drove past the next day was that of a sort of bandstand wired together from cake racks, each painted a different color—more an "atrocity" than, say, a folly.

It was the simple words that threw me. Right after the bought-vote-dentistry story we got onto the subject of bears. Chubby's ancestors include a fair number of men who worked with the vast livestock herds that dominated the landscape on the plateau before the passage of the Taylor Grazing Act in 1934. Back then grizzly bears still raided the plains from their fortresses in the high ranges, taking their tithe from the stockmen. Though the grizzly is gone, brown black bears remain, protected in part from the high-country villagers by their old cousin's goblin reputation. Chub was telling me how dangerous a bear ("berr")—or at least a "roog berr"—could be, how it would appropriate a deer or elk kill and stand its ground. "I know," he said. "Besides, my dad used to be a cheap cheerer, and he had a lot of experience with berrs."

"Cheap cheerer?" All I could think of was the past hour's tales of political chicanery. "What does a cheap cheerer do?"

Chubby looked at me as though I were out of my mind. "A cheap cheerer cheers cheap!" With visions of packed political rallies full of country villagers bought for a quarter a head, I still stared until he began to make stripping motions with one hand against another that clutched an invisible large object. "Cheap cheerer, cheap cheerer! He cuts the wool off!"

In those first few months we met a couple of people who were to shape our perceptions as much as the land. I met the first as a brusque, nervous voice on the phone. "You know about hawks? I got this old hawk I caught. It's been eatin' my game chickens. Dutch Salmon tells me you know how to train 'em."

I was cautious. Falconry is difficult, demanding, and romantic, attracting many dilettantes as well as the potentially dedicated and, without a felled forest of bureaucratic permits both state and federal, illegal. The voice sounded like an old Hank Williams record, seriously country. What to ask?

"Uh, what's it look like?"

"A goshawk." Score one for the voice—most people don't know a hawk from a handsaw, and all I had been looking for was something basic, like what color it was, not a species identification.

"How'd you catch it?" Maybe he had used a steel trap and broken its legs; game chickens, after all, are expensive.

"On a bunch of nooses tied to a screen. He killed seventeen so far, but he's too damn pretty to shoot. I finally decided I could catch him—he ain't shy."

Better and better. "You know it's illegal to have one without permits?"

I couldn't decide whether the voice sounded irritated or amused or (with hindsight) a little of both. "I'm not planning on getting a damn license for him. I'll probably just let him go on the other side of the mountain. But he's real neat—he'll already come across the room to a dead chicken on my hand. I thought you might like to see him."

And so I drove out the seventy miles on the pavement and down the twenty miles more of dirt road to meet John and Becky Davila. In their twenties, they lived in unlikely elegance in John's father's house, amidst books and pine-panelled walls, surrounded by cars, trucks, an eighteen-wheeler, a motorcycle, fighting chickens, and peafowl. John was tall and thin and pale, with a long, mournful El Greco face, a hawk's nose, and a cowboy twang that fit his style and roper's buckle, if not his name. Born on the ranch out of a pure New Mexican Hispano, highly educated background, he dropped out of school to ride rodeo and never went back. His hard-core redneck image can slip an inch or two when he talks about being in a boat off Belize (on a gold-hunting expedition) or when he does a New Jersey accent he picked up when he was there with a Wild West show (he stayed with cousins in Manhattan). But in general it's a good defense against outsiders' condescension. "You ought to hear them hippies down in Reserve when I talk about Meskins and Indians. And then they see Beck."

Becky's mother was Navajo, her father Pete a Jack Mormon cowboy from Idaho, bearded like the prophet. She is tall and graceful with long black hair and Indian bone structure in her face. John is restless and excitable. Becky is sane and serene and reads books. John can't speak a word of Spanish. Back when illegal-alien labor was still common in the high country, it was Beck who would deal with those polite and desperate people.

John showed me the gos, an old male with a steel blue back and eyes like garnets, already willing to eat on his fist. We agreed to let it go about two mountain ranges over. It had already eaten about five hundred dollars' worth of adolescent gamefowl. They invited us to dinner, where for one moment I feared that I had put my foot in it. "What's this?" I asked as I spooned up a morsel from a bowl of stew laced with green chile. "Meat," said John without a smile. But the conversation soared again, fired by "Old Bobwire"—white bootleg whiskey in which red chilies had been soaked. By the time we left John and Beck had agreed to visit over the intervening ninety miles, in a week or two, and meet us at Old Jonay's Bar in Quemado for the street dance and fiesta.

Two days later I got up from my desk to a knocking at the door. A short, athletic Anglo in his late fifties, wearing tinted glasses, stood in the doorway. "Excuse me," he said. "I know this is a dumb question. But do you really have a falcon?"

"Yes." I felt the reluctance again.

"I'm Floyd Mansell. You've got some fine dogs, too." Floyd could not have known it, but Chubby Torres had already recommended "Mr. Mansell" to us as someone who kept hunting dogs and gamefowl and spent time in the backcountry.

I asked him in. As he later admitted, Floyd was out to demonstrate that he knew a bit more about natural history than an average small-town teacher. Before he sat down, he had identified the print on the wall as a gyrfalcon, and commented on an old Ernest Thompson Seton book that lay on the coffee table of planks and cinder blocks in our improvised living room. "I hardly dared believe you had a real hawk. I figured it was a tame raven, or worse."

We showed Floyd the hawk, and offered him a drink, which he refused, then coffee, which he accepted. In the next three hours we touched on hawks (he knew where there was a Cooper's hawk nest in the San Mateo mountains thirty miles to the west), on snakes (he had extended the known range of the Mojave rattler for several hundred miles with a specimen he had collected), on bow hunting, black powder, hounds, and game chickens. We also got a little autobiography. A self-described hillbilly from Arkansas (although half Lebanese), Floyd had left home at seventeen to join the Navy. After seeing heavy action in the Pacific he came back to attend college on the GI Bill. He would eventually achieve a master's degree; meanwhile, in his own words, he "became a Catholic, turned liberal, married an Indian, and moved to New Mexico. My family still doesn't know what to think of me."

In the thirty or so years he had spent in New Mexico, Floyd had been a mayor, the principal of two schools, a guidance counselor, a coach, and at least a minor power in the Democratic party. He had worked for the local fire service, drilled wells, collected snakes and arrowheads, and fought conservation battles. He had also kept up the three sporting passions he had inherited from his father, a hard man, a Baptist and a bootlegger: hounds, boxing and cockfighting. Too, he had somehow found the time to share in the raising of nine children.

Quemado is the last stop on Route 60, almost all the way to Arizona; with a population of about five hundred, it is also the largest town in Catron County. Its name means "burnt." Tony Hillerman, New Mexico's finest novelist, says, not at all obliquely, "This was just a little dinky place . . . and it didn't even have a name. Then one morning Geronimo and his Apaches came riding through and after that they took to calling it Quemado."

Something of the mood still lingers; Magdalena these days is a tiny center, determinedly respectable, while Quemado ironically cherishes the reputation of being the wild-ass cowtown that Magdalena once really was.

The fiesta and street dance was in full swing, and Quemado was roaring. A country band played in one bar, loud enough to be heard in the other. Young men in tall hats, with one boot spurred, ambled through the streets eyeing slender girls in tight jeans and drinking beer from paper cups. When I poked my head into Jonay's I saw John, resplendent in a silver-belly Resistol hat, a black shirt with pearl buttons, and python boots. I waved and he turned to the bar, to emerge in a moment with a go-cup of Jack Daniels for me. "This is getting out of hand."

"Have you seen Dutch?"

"Yeah. He's heading out. He and Kathy finally broke up. He's got twenty dogs in his truck and trailer. They're going to Roswell tonight."

I couldn't believe it. One of the reasons we settled here was the distant but real presence of Dutch, who was sort of an easterner and most definitely a writer; therefore, an interpreter and buffer between us and the Real West.

"Roswell?"

"Yeah. About five or six hours east of you; out past Ruidoso."

A moment later Dutch himself appeared. He didn't seem too grim but his jaw was set. "I don't want to see Mangas again. I don't want to talk about it." His truck contained his whole motley pack. They set up a chorus of howls and yodels as we approached. We had just backed off for the sake of our eardrums when another ruckus broke out behind us.

The middle of Route 60, which had just seconds before contained only a few wandering bodies, now held a brawl as thick as a snarl of ants on a summer sidewalk. Above the thwack of fists against bodies rose a cry I will never forget: *"That horse never fucked nobody!"* John and I started forward in happy fascination. As I drained my drink, flipped the cup over my shoulder, and sped off I felt a hand on my collar. I spun around to see Betsy grinning at Becky. "He doesn't have any good sense either. I think he's worked bars too long."

I retreated, sheepishly. A line of cars and recreation vehicles with Iowa plates was beginning to back up behind the brawl; the honks of the tourists and the whinnying of horses rose over the shouts. Dutch had started his engine. "Adios!" He backed and filled, angling the trailer until he could turn his truck back toward the east. I protested that I had just wanted to see, while the women exchanged knowing grins. John, shaking his head, went for another drink as the police began to wade into the fray. The Annual Quemado Street Dance and Brawl was almost over, and we were on our own.

IV

With Dutch gone, we faced New Mexico with a mixture of anticipation and dread, like brand-new graduates dropped into the real world. The last snows melted. Mud turned to iron and then to dust. Almost before the mud dried in deep ruts on the village streets, the wind started. It blew twenty-five, thirty, forty miles per hour, steady enough to lean on, straight out of the west for days at a time. If we drove out to the Davila's, heading upstream, it would force us down to thirty at the top of every hill. By April winter's clouds had vanished, but the sun's heat was still modified by the wind, even filtered by the dust the wind raised. In May, the weather turned clear and still and hot.

This is the weather Albuquerque forecasters love. "Another fair warm day," they chirp (do only weathermen use "fair" as an adjective describing weather?), "ninety degrees Fahrenheit, sunny, no rain." I hated it. Although high-country New Mexico never featured the enervating heat of Arizona or the south or even coastal Massachusetts, there was something inimical about the weather in May and June. It was so dry that my nose bled; my lips cracked and my eyes got red even if I didn't drink the night before. Betsy slathered on oil, but she loved the sun. Before this, her favorite places had included Mexico and the south of Spain, and she was amused by my distress.

As the wind died and the heat came on, I went to the foothills, and walked for miles every afternoon in the juniper barrens north of town. I wore a straw cowboy hat and sunglasses against the glare, carried nothing heavier than binoculars. The utter strangeness of the environment, its lack of familiar details, oppressed me: the dryness, the lack of songbirds, the unrelieved sun and cloudless, dark blue sky. In the mountains, or driving along the plains, I could fool myself about where I was, but not here. The scant grass was brown and bitten to ground level by cattle, the footing jumbled lava rock that clanked like broken bottles. Arroyos cut the ground every few hundred yards, sometimes too wide to jump. The juniper burned dark vivid green; the bright patches hurt my eyes even through the glasses, while the shadows were black and unnaturally cold. Weird insects hung in the air as lizards sprinted away, flexing their backbones, right, left, right. If I saw any bird it was likely to be the prehistoric silhouette of a roadrunner, peering suspiciously from beneath its shaggy curls. I would go home uneasy, as though I had not walked at all.

The sunsets were strange too, luminous and still, with no drama but a wonderful glow. One evening Betsy went out to watch and came back in about thirty seconds saying something like: *"Theresasnakeimperfectlycalmimnottalkingfast!"*

There was *asnake*, not the first we had seen in the country, nor the biggest, but the first we had seen leaning against the house. It was a prairie rattler, a stout two-footer in dusty brown, and it was buzzing almost comically. Big diamondbacks sound metallic and dangerous, but this one made a noise like a toy. Betsy had apparently seen it while passing over its head; whether or not it had struck at her was unclear, as she was attempting to photograph it with the lens cover still on even as she denied being excited. "Nonsense. It's a darling snake!"

Snakes, which I have always kept, might have been the one area in our lives where I was more competent and calmer than Betsy. I carried out a trash can and lifted the irritable little viper into it with a jack handle. As I released it at the abandoned airport she took a photo: smiling me, three-foot bar, fat dangling sausage of snake, with its rattle cocked at a jaunty angle. Later, we made a card out of the photo. We called it "Cleaning the Yard in the Land of Enchantment."

The still, hot days stayed and stayed. I felt encased in molten glass, bored and nervous. I had nothing to do but walk, and walking was never enough. Betsy had better ideas. Knowing how long it takes for an alien land to accept you, she busied herself working our new "long dog" pups in the yard.

Within a month of our arrival we had taken home two pups from Dutch's kennel. Prematurely grizzled Riley, named after a ghost town to the north, was a cross between a male greyhound and a Scottish deerhound bitch, although at seven weeks he more resembled a horrifying mixture of monkey and tarantula. He was all legs and knobby joints and thin, black fur, with a sharp muzzle, tiny eyes, and huge, white teeth. His formidable appearance was belied by his sweet timid temperament; he spent most of his first three months hiding under the couch from spaniels, visitors, and his partner.

Luna, his foster brother and running mate, was grave, comely, and arrogant, a perfectly proportioned miniature saluki one week older than Riley. Although a third smaller, his greatest pleasure in life seemed to be in tormenting his hapless sibling.

They began to chase things almost as soon as we brought them home. Coursing dogs are natural athletes and instinctive hunters. They need no incentive or training beyond the necessary civilizing minimum, and, in the case of salukis, they don't accept that much. If a weed seed blew through the yard or a butterfly flut-tered low, they were after it like twin shadows, coordinating so well that Betsy named their moves "synchronized dogging," after the Olympic swimming event. And if a rabbit dared browse out of the patches of yucca and rabbit brush outside the pen, they'd go mad with joy and lust, standing on their hind legs, whining, holding on to the wire with what Chubby called their hands.

Betsy's training consisted of letting them chase cottontails, which gave the puppies short runs before the rabbits disappeared down their holes, and in calling them across fences so they learned how to deal with barbed wire. They were still too young to chase hares. A jackrabbit would not only run away with them and dis-courage them, it might do irreparable damage to growing tissues as they tried to catch up. Besides, a sighthound could run itself to death under the summer sun. We heard horror stories of eager dogs dead in an instant of heat stroke, or others whose back mus-cles disintegrated. "They ran their backs off," as the phrase went. If you wanted your dog to have had enough aerobic exercise to catch anything by the time winter brought real running, you had to start in the cool of the high-desert night, when temperatures dropped thirty or forty degrees from the midafternoon high.

But how to find quarry at night amid the calling poorwills, hunting rattlers, skunks and porcupines? And how to chase it then? "Sighthound" is not an arbitrary term; greyhounds and sa-lukis and deerhounds are as visual as humans, and chase only what they see.

Betsy called Floyd. It turned out that he had already started his conditioning runs in the dark using spotlights. On the plain I would walk for five hours under the weight of the sun without seeing anything move but a scuttling earless lizard or a tilting vulture. But after dark, the thirty-section "pastures" of the cattle range came alive.

Betsy wrote a letter to a friend. "I went out with Floyd, Riley, two young dogs, Marley and Gates, and scarred black and white Blaze, a veteran of coyote and badger. We drove in the dog truck which has two boxes, one on each side, where the pickup bed ought to be. Gates across the sides let the dogs hang their heads over to see what there is to see on the dark nights Floyd favors. Behind the cab, standing on the spare tire between the cab and dog boxes, is Brandon, Floyd's thirteen-year-old son, with a spotlight in his hand."

"Slowly, we drive down the dirt road across the flat pastureland. I peer out my side as the spot sweeps across, Floyd peers out his side in the night. Suddenly thunderous banging on the roof of the cab says Brandon has spotted a jackrabbit. I yank the wire behind my shoulder as Floyd yanks his, the gates fly open and the four big sighthounds hit the dirt, charging for the light which is moving with the jack. Then the quarry is gone, over a slight rise, out of the light. Lost. Brandon switches off his light, and the dogs spring huge into the headlights looking hopefully down the cones of light for something that moves. Nothing.

"We load them back into their boxes, and drive slowly to a cattle tank. Along the road Brandon thumps again. Yank on the wire, huge shadows of dogs bounding through the darkness, white Gates just visible. The jackrabbit sits perfectly still in the spotlight about twenty feet from the pickup. The dogs run by, not seeing or identifying its still body as quarry. They are out there, thundering down the headlit road. We look at the jack, he at us and then slowly, slowly, he moves out of the light, into the safe darkness.

"Out with the spotlight, then on with the headlights and the hounds return. You hear them before seeing them and brace against a possible collision. The moon is up now, and though their bodies are invisible, two bright lights at about head level show. I ask Floyd if he has sewn reflectors on their collars.

"He laughs. 'It's their eyes, Betsy, their eyes!' They're all around us now, nosing for a pat, sides heaving from the run. We grasp their collars, and guide their grinning, panting selves back to the boxes. Load 'em up, drive on to the tank.

"There, plenty waits. Seven jackrabbits spaced out on the flat beaten circle around the tank. 'Get the closest,' yells Floyd, and Brandon's light searches. They're on it.

"The rabbit takes off in great leaping strides, four dogs close behind. They race in the light, for this jack shows that suicidal tendency of his kind in preferring to stay in the light. He jinks, and the dogs lose advantage; then wise old Blaze and Riley surge forward. Riley lunges and the jack turns sharply left into the jaws of Blaze. 'Textbook perfect,' says Floyd.

"We load them up again, and just before the gate swings shut on him Blaze jumps out and jogs purposefully over to the tank for a drink. We let the others out and they join him jostling, satisfied, amiable. Then one by one they jog back to the pickup for the ride home. The rabbit will be chili by tomorrow night."

Luna's first kill was a quail. A covey erupted in front of him as he trotted beside me, not even hunting; their explosive flush triggered him into an improbable leap and chop that ended with him spread-eagled over a bush, the fluttering quail winding down like a spring toy in his mouth.

He was horrified. The spaniels would literally rather retrieve, or as the canine behaviorists say, "object-carry," than eat; the mere possibility of a "fetch" drives them to wiggle on the ground like cats stoned on catnip. But Luna was so appalled by the vibrating feather pillow in his mouth that he ran in three hysterical circles and spat it out at my feet. *Paah!* As I tucked the bird furtively into my pocket—it was a month until quail season—he stood on his head and wiped his mouth on the grass. Finally he sneezed twice, explosively, looking me in the eye as though it were my fault. He never touched a bird again.

Riley killed a bird once, years later, with about as much intent. I can't resist a couple of lines from Betsy's letter to a friend: "They returned, and Floyd took them to a tank where to his enormous surprise they got something. Namely a mallard. Gates, who caught the duck, seemed nonplussed and trotted off and buried it. Riley dug it up again ("Dante Gabriel Rosetti / buried all of his libretti / thought the matter over, then / went and dug them up again'), and brought it in to Floyd, quite alive, quite unhurt. Floyd cracked it over the head and put it in the back of the pickup, whereupon it got up and flew back to the tank where Riley caught it again and done it in. 'Coursing for Duck on the Western Plains—A New Method.' "

Bigger quarry beckoned, though Riley, a coyote dog, would not be seasoned enough for his real work for another year and a half. As the pups gained strength and the daytime temperature cooled we began to take them to the edge of the San Augustine Plains, where the grass stretched to the horizon. We'd walk for hours, the dogs trotting beside us or galloping ahead, rolling up out of the scrub like porpoises when they hit a patch of rabbit brush. We were looking for hares. But one day a buck antelope seemed to materialize from the thin air, trotting ahead of the pups. They blurred into a full-out run like a still picture turning into a movie. I could almost hear the whipcrack of Riley's spine. His feet thudded against the ground, raising car-sized clouds of dust as the runners cut across our path. The antelope did not seem to be making an effort yet. His black-horned head was erect as he bounced along, feet together, although his mouth was open to supercharge his blood with oxygen. Luna, running with similar ease, ghosted along to the rear. Riley was flat-out, flexing like a cheetah, just behind the buck's heels. But even as we watched he began to slow. As he fell back Luna, a grey and white wraith, spaced fifty yards behind the bouncing white spots of the antelope, faded with the quarry into the dusty horizon like a boat into the ocean on a hazy day. I started down the track, but it was an hour before I found him. He was walking—not trotting, but walking slowly, limping on all four feet, tongue dragging just above the dust. He must have run twelve miles. I picked him up and slung him across my shoulders. He did not object but lay there panting as I walked out to the truck.

The pups were to use this one-two punch—Riley sprinting, testing the quarry, Luna pressing on to the finish—with much greater effect on hares. Antelope, especially parties of young bucks, continued to plague us. Oddly—hunters find them hard to stalk—they would come in, heads high, scatter wildly as I yelled and waved my hat at them, then sneak back to watch again. But by constant vigilance I managed to keep them beyond the dogs' critical "flight distance."

Our entrance to coyote coursing was ambiguous. I maintain an unease, bordering on an aversion, to killing any coyote. This is not a moral stricture; the only methods of coyote-killing I consider wrong are the absolutely unfair, taxpayer-funded government helicopter "hunts," and poisoning. Betsy, who was at least as kind as I, was more realistic. She wrote to a friend: "We find ourselves ambivalent about [the coyote's] death, particularly Steve who rather identifies with predators. I don't know 'bout that. If either of us were as good predators as your run-of-the-mill coyote I might feel greater kinship. As it is, I sort of tip my eyebrow at him if I see him (not having a suitable hat or sex for tipping that, and it not being my nature to curtsy without a suitable skirt) and feel, well, if he loses, he loses, just like you or me."

Such nonchalance vanishes when you ride the dog truck. A coyote chase is sublime, frightening for both chaser and chased, a combination of pity, fear for your own life, hunter's desire, and dog's art—a thrill and a small tragedy, all in one. The first time we went coyote hunting we rode for three long hours over the empty plain in the ancient orange flat-bed with its dog boxes perched high up behind the cab, plunging over the tussocks like a small boat in a heavy sea. Then Floyd spied a patch of different brown against the plain's lion tan, about six hundred yards out. Without even a "there's one!" he slowed the pickup around and plunged into the bottom of an arroyo. As we surged up the wave of earth on the other side, unable to see anything but sky through the windshield, he managed to say, "Get ready to pull that chain!" Then we were diving again, tires spitting dirt and accelerating. Ahead, a creature that looked just like our yellow town dog Winnie had begun to jog away, looking back over "her" shoulder. (I could not escape the identification.)

"We're all going to die." This from Betsy, who was sitting between Floyd and me, digging her nails into my—and despite her and his propriety, Floyd's—thigh. When we hit forty miles per hour Floyd tugged on his chain. I pulled mine and the butterfly doors popped open with a loud clunk. The dogs hit running.

They edged ahead as we slowed for another arroyo, throwing up clods and puffs of dust. I imagined I could hear their pounding feet even over the straining engine and Betsy's sudden whole-hearted cowboy whoop, "Yee *hah!*" The coyote looked back again, seemed to stretch her gallop—and then vanished, gone where the light goes when you flip the switch to off. We all charged on for a few seconds more, but she had taken advantage of a fold in the ground, ducked, trotted at right angles to the chase for a few yards and gone to ground. The run was over.

The dogs stood, sides heaving, heads hanging as though dragged down by their heavy tongues. Floyd looked rueful. I hope that my grinning face concealed my real relief that this one time the coyote had won, just like you or me. Betsy was ecstatic; she had found her sport, and her personal animals. For the rest of her life she would talk of hounds' beauty to uncomprehending friends, dream of a horse she could ride to follow them, and settle for the truck. In my favorite photo of her she holds the collars of the saluki and the gaunt staghound. A white scarf hangs to her waist. Her hair is windblown, and she is smiling, aware of nothing but her pride in the dogs.

With cooling weather came more possibilities for adventure and embarrassment. I was a shotgunner and bird hunter, by definition an effete easterner. If you don't hunt, the idea that any hunter might be thought effete by his peers might seem strange. If your image of the shooter comes from television, you think that a shotgun sprays a ten-foot-wide death zone. I have had a serious, intelligent urbanite ask me why, if I am such a sportsman, I don't use a rifle on flying birds. Apart from that the impact of a heavy, high-velocity bullet would vaporize a bird whose meat is one of earth's finest products, I don't because I want my shooting to be difficult, a test of skill, rather than impossible. A successful wing shot must hit a target the size of a softball that is racing away at about forty-five miles per hour, with a handful of lead spheres that are smaller than BB's. The pattern spreads to about three feet in width before it loses so much velocity that it will not penetrate the bird; at the usual distance, there are often holes in it big enough for the bird to fly through. You can't even aim at the bird; rather, you must sweep the barrels of your gun along, pointing them at an imagined spot where the bird will be, a distance that is different for every shot. Wingshooting is harder than tennis, more abstract than chess, and more complicated than baseball. It requires time and skill, and the only reward is a few, tiny birds.

It was September 1st, the premier opening day in New Mexico: dove season. I wanted advice. In New England a combination of Puritanism, sentimentality, and urbanization has combined to declare the mourning dove—the smallest, fastest, most abundant and difficult of all upland game—a songbird. No Puritan could endure shooting twenty-five shells and missing twenty of the shots in order to bring home four—the dog ate one—four-ounce birds. I knew nothing about doves—where to find them, what they ate, how to hit them. And I was in the backcountry of the West, where we had been led to believe that nobody would deign to burn powder on anything that didn't have split hooves and horns.

I swallowed my pride and called Chubby. "You ever hunt doves?"

"Sometimes. But I don't have a shotgun."

"Where? I mean, what kind of places do you find them in?"

"At tanks. I'll show you."

What with writing and dog training, I wasn't ready to go when he arrived. I handed him a 20-gauge side-by-side double-barreled gun. He had never used such a weapon, being more familiar with pump shotguns—the kind you see in crime shows where a slide works under a single barrel, *ka-chunk!*—than my old-fashioned, vaguely European tool. But when I gave him a box of shells, and showed him how it broke open when the top lever was thumbed to the right, he drove away looking satisfied.

He returned a few days later with a present of ten cleaned doves. "How was the gun?" I asked.

"It shoots good," was his typically laconic reply. "I even got three on one shot." This seemed odd, but I assumed they bunched up as they came in. A couple of weeks later I was attempting to write and getting nowhere when Chubby came by again. "Want to hunt some doves?"

I assumed this was in part a request for a shotgun. I handed Chubby my pump 12-gauge and took the light double. We were headed into the juniper scrublands north of town five minutes later, and soon were crouched under a massive cottonwood beside the tank, a circular galvanized iron artificial pond, like an enormous kid's wading pool. Such cattle tanks, served by windmills, shaded by trees that grow on the overflow, are the only permanent standing water in mesa country. Everything comes to them to drink. Dragonflies whirred, swallows dipped, lizards stopped and started. At first, my eyes followed every songbird, but soon I drowsed. It was Chubby who muttered, "Here they come."

I looked around frantically but saw nothing. Then they were fluttering, braking with a whistle of wings. My first shot went wide, but my second puffed feathers and brought a bird down in a slanting glide toward a purple patch of turkey pea. It took several minutes to find it. As I bent to pick it up I heard wings and crouched, fumbling in the pocket of my camo shirt for shells.

They swung in a circle but Chubby held his fire. As they curved around again I stood, swung, fired, and missed with both barrels. The afternoon went on in similar manner. Doves would come, I would fire, I would miss, and Chubby would sit like an Indian statue.

On the next party I held my fire. Six doves landed and began to drink. Chubby moved around to my left, lined up the big pump like a rifle, and fired into their midst. "Four!" he said with a grin.

"Uh, we usually shoot them flying."

"That's why you miss."

We wanted to live here, and, more subtly, to do things that would connect us to the landscape. With these mixed motives in mind, and because we were falconers—which is to say members of a semi-esoteric, exclusive brotherhood linked by shared passions and arcane knowledge—we called the nearest falconer. Not only was Jim Skidmore someone we knew we could talk to on at least one subject, we wanted a western bird.

"A western bird," a phrase taken for granted by falconers, can itself describe the land if you understand it. In the East, the Midwest, or the sodden jungles of the Pacific Northwest, visibility is limited by what gets in the way. There, you'll want a goshawk or red-tail, a broad-winged hawk of the forest that will ride on your fist and chase such things as rabbits for a short distance before she kills, returns, or lands in a tree to await your flush. But in the West you can see the horizon. Here, you'll want a true falcon—a rare peregrine, an arctic cyr, a native prairie—to stand on the wind overhead and chase down quarry as swift as she is. Long wings demand long sights.

Jim, a born westerner, had never condescended to fly a plebian "shortwing." In fact, his last twenty years had been spent in service to three female peregrines. His whole life had been devoted to falconry; he regarded his stints in the Air Force, in teaching, and, now, as a pharmaceutical salesman, as nothing more than support systems for his birds. An earlier marriage had broken up over Jim's dedication, and he later told us that his wife had suggested that he go screw his birds as she left. Birds had determined where he lived, his schedule, what trucks he owned. They had driven him to buy an Airstream trailer to use on the plains "grouse camps," to breed pointers, and to learn how to use a sewing machine to make bags and packs for equipment. He had the enthusiast's innocent belief that everyone shared his level of obsession. After an evening looking at two hundred slides of Jim's three identical peregrines, Betsy swore she could tell them apart.

Prairie falcons are very particular in their nesting requirements. They demand cliffs, high and vertical enough to be inaccessible to predators, and they prefer southern exposures. In a land as big as New Mexico, such sites are still few and far between, but Jim seemed to know every one, and to be determined to take us to all of them. Falcon-nesting became our way into the map, translating abstract lines into reality.

This, again, was different from anything we had ever seen before. The first time we went out with Jim we drove forty miles east of the mountains, where the high plains are as big as the ocean, and stopped at a highway rest area. The ground was as flat as a floor, sparsely vegetated with junipers. I couldn't see a cliff, or for that matter an anthill, but shut my mouth and followed, carrying a coil of climber's rope around my shoulder. We hopped the fence and started walking. The day was hot and smelled of dust. Jim rambled on about nests he had visited and I drank Gatorade and wondered what the hell we were doing. Then he stopped. "It should be around here. Maybe bear a little to the right."

I felt as though the rules of the universe had changed. I could see nothing but ten-foot, dark-green trees, separated by bitten-down dead grass and sand. We lurched ahead for another hundred yards, Jim quickening his pace, and emerged on the edge of a cliff that stretched left and right as far as the eye could see below our feet. I am slightly acrophobic. I can deal with heights if I work up to them slowly, but get dizzy if I come upon them with no warning. This was so unexpected that I simply sat down.

Jim grinned and gestured. "It's right across that bay there." The cliff cut back to my left. Across the bay, about ten feet below the lip, was a hole with a spaghetti-like cluster of white streaks hanging from its edge: "noodles," falcon droppings. But the whole spectacle was even more impressive than my first sight of a New Mexico aerie and I turned from the nest to look at ranch buildings a half-mile away and a couple of hundred feet below, to a ribbon of cliffs across the basin that must reflect the ones we were sitting on, to a horizon which seemed farther away than the sea. This wasn't home, and I liked it just fine.

The nest was empty. Two great black eagles standing still on the air that blew up over the lip of the cliff, slope soaring in silent menace, must have caused the nervous falcons to move. In retrospect, the absence of falcons at that first nest was good for us. We began to feel western distances as we searched aeries "only" eighty miles away, to know what landforms corresponded with cryptic marks on the topo maps. By the time we finally located a nest on a breaking wave of sandstone that faced southwest over the jagged black moonscape of lava malpais near Grants, we had learned a little more about driving to the horizon.

And then we got invited to the chicken fights.

Cockfighting is not something New Englanders talk about, though it is more popular there than you might think. Floyd, not knowing my attitudes, was at first rather diffident about his game fowl. When I expressed interest, he was delighted. These were birds to be proud of—big, upstanding roosters that shook down their shining, hard, jeweled feathers with a loud rattle. Each stalked about at the end of a leash, commanding a circle of ground about twelve feet in diameter. Their heads, "dubbed," or trimmed of wattle when they were chicks, had a snaky dinosaurian look. Their brilliant eyes observed everything as they paced the ground on sturdy legs with square-cut spur stubs.

They were tame. When we approached they did not dart about

in the usual mad chicken's fashion, but stood their ground. When Floyd lifted one with a hand beneath its belly it lay passive, legs dangling, looking as though it would go to sleep on his arm. He stroked the lancelike red hackles on its neck and they shimmered in the late-afternoon light. These were the feathers desired by trout fishermen to make the finest dryflies, a stiff, iridescent ruff that would spread like a cobra's head at the sight of a challenger.

Floyd explained the birds' docility—cockfighters disapprove of "manfighting" birds and so handle their gladiators constantly to keep them tame. A five-pound bird armed with the metal gaff that trained cocks wear over their spurs could be a daunting handful were it not tame. He showed me the gaffs, three-inch, hand-crafted steel spurs with sharp points but no edges, elegant as fine swords, and told me the cockfighter's rationale for their use. Before gaffs were invented, cockfights might go on for hours, wearing down both combatants to the point of no return—a sort of death of ten thousand cuts. Now a clean kill or clean victory is more common. He also produced sparring muffs, tiny padded boxing gloves that attached to the spurs in the same manner as the gaffs, for use in bloodless practice bouts.

I was taken by all this recondite lore and eighteenth-century art. I found myself wanting to see a fight, though I couldn't say why. I was worried about Betsy's attitude, and realized that what she thought about the subject meant a lot to me. The result of the sixties' "letting it all hang out" had taught me reticence about things that mattered. Would the lady from Boston approve of such a barbarous sport? She had walked through Floyd's demonstration and had asked a few intelligent questions, but had given no sign of approval or disapproval. Looking for one, I struggled aloud to defend something that really didn't bother my conscience at all. I quoted the English writer George Ryley Scott, in *The History of Cockfighting*: "The case against so many other sports is that the hunters only are willing." I cited the naturalist-explorer Hume, who discovered a sort of cockpit built by red junglefowl, the gamecock's ancestor, in Borneo: "Whilst I was looking around, one of my dogs brought me from somewhere in the jungle round a freshly killed Junglecock, in splendid plumage, but with the base of the skull on one side pierced by what I at once concluded must have been the spur of another cock—on speaking to the men, found that they knew the place well, and one of them said that he had repeatedly watched the cocks fighting there."

She laughed at me, though gently. "Love, my grandfather kept fighting cocks." She told me for the first time about that fierce old man. Her father, bishop and gentle socialist, was already so removed from me in time—born in 1867, died the year I was born—that I had never considered her grandfather, Colonel Robert, who fought in Cuba with Roosevelt and later became commandant of the Marine Corps. He retired toward the end of the last century and bought a plantation in Charlottesville, Virginia. "He died long before I was thought of."

"So how do you know about his chickens, for Christ's sake? Doesn't sound like your regular family lore."

"Did I ever tell you about George?"

"Probably." She had so many tales of so many people, most referred to by first names only, that I could get lost.

"George's mother's ghastly parents were so determined that she marry someone proper that they bought her a plantation in Virginia. George told me they bought it from an old southern colonel's widow. 'What was it called?' I asked. 'Moriah,' says he. I told

STEPHEN BODIO

him, 'That colonel was not southern. That colonel was my grandfather from Connecticut.' We called George's mother, and she said yes indeed it had been bought from Mrs. Huntington, and came complete with the colonel's pair of greys and his stable of fighting cocks."

"So?"

"So let's go to the chicken fights."

John Davila had six stags, yearling cocks ready for their first fight. He agreed to take us to the big legal pit north of us on the river. On a chilly Saturday morning we met at the Lotaburger stand and followed John and Beck to a prefab barn that stood alone in an expanse of grassy mesa east of town. It was surrounded by vehicles, ranging from typical New Mexican trucks to a couple of fancy German and Japanese sedans. Children ran about in the sandy lot and men stood in knots sipping brown-bag whiskey. Inside the windowless barn the only light came from fluorescent bulbs in the corners and over the pit, a sand-floored ring about eighteen feet wide, enclosed in a cage and surrounded by gymnasium-style bleachers. The crowd was heterogeneous, even for New Mexico, and its components looked less depraved than the average sports fan on television. Kids were everywhere, chasing each other through the stands, screeching in English and Spanish and a couple of Indian languages.

A man whom I could only imagine to be the master of ceremonies entered the cage and shut the iron door behind him with a clang. He was blond and neatly mustached, dressed in a perfect straw Stetson with a pearl-buttoned red shirt and an immense silver and turquoise belt, and carried a cane in his hand. He cleared his throat and gestured with the cane, turning and smiling until everyone shut up. "Good morning, ladies and gentlemen, and welcome. Before we begin this morning I want to remind you of two small things. First of all, cockfighting is a family sport. So if you want to drink, do it outside. Second, as you all know, it is illegal to gamble on cockfights in New Mexico! So remember, no betting!" ("He has to say that," whispered John.) "Now, the first fight today is. . . ." As he announced the names, two cockfighters excuse-me'd through the crowd with their contestants tucked under their arms. One was a tall Anglo in his mid-forties; his bird, a "pile," was pale in color with blurred streaks of red, like watercolors over a white base. The other cocker was a broad-faced Indian youth with a classic, iridescent red-over-black bird, the most primitive and beautiful color of domestic fowl.

In the pit, the master of ceremonies—actually, I was informed, the judge—was drawing parallel lines in the sand with his cane. The cockers crouched, allowing their birds to see one another above their elbows. "Bill your cocks!" Now they leaned closer together, heads almost touching, as they allowed the birds to spar with quick grabs of their heads. Then, without orders, they retreated behind the lines to hold the birds by their tails, feet on the ground, still with a cautious hand across the birds' breasts. Each bird dug in his feet like a runner, straining against restraint.

"Pit your cocks!" The birds ran straight into each other, heads low and encircled by bristling ruffs, and exploded into a blur of motion which in less than a second resolved itself into frozen sculpture: the pile down, wing outstretched, the red above with spur embedded in the pile's wing, heads erect, eyes glowing with mindless fury. The crowd roared and I stared in puzzlement, not sure what had happened. The cockers danced around the birds as the judge ordered, "handle!" They slipped hands beneath their birds, quickly, gently, detached the hung-up spur, and retreated without a word.

John was sportscasting. "Doesn't mean a thing, those wing cuts—either could win—the red goes high, and that's good—they're both game, no runners—watch 'em now—he's spitting water on the pile's head to revive it—okay, they're coming back!"

The judge checked his watch, looked up. "Get ready. Okay gentlemen, pit your cocks!"

This time they circled like deadly dancers, as beautiful as snakes. They came together in the air, flying, holding themselves up against gravity as they struck savage boxer's blows at each other's chests. Though it seemed to take a long time, it was most likely about thirty seconds before they were hopelessly entangled. The pile, the lower bird, looked seriously bedraggled. I asked John. "Yep. He took a couple of serious hits."

"Handle. Thirty seconds."

The pile's handler lifted him up with a hand under his chest so that his legs dangled. John whispered to me, "That's dumb. He's taking weight off the bird's legs that way, but putting pressure on its chest—makes it harder for him to breathe."

"Pit your cocks!"

The birds stalked in, posturing warily. Then the red fired up into the air and came prancing down in a deadly shuffle. The pile bucked, reared, subsided, quivered, and died. The red staggered back and gave a prolonged, gurgling crow. It was over.

The fight had gone so fast I had to wait until it was done to think about what I had felt. It had been barbaric and bloody, but so beautiful I hadn't noticed the pain until the end, and so exciting that I knew I had been cheering aloud with all the others.

Betsy, uninterested as always in self-justification, never said another word about whether watching gamefowl fight was good or bad. We continued to attend, helped Floyd run his own yearly games, and took many photos, the only good ones I have ever seen on the subject. (Here an advantage to running a local cockfight. A friend from L. A. was nearly assaulted for trying to do the same at the legal pit.)

About two years later, Betsy wrote to eastern friends uncomfortable with our *aficion*. "Where once my grandfather lived is now a housing development. *Sic transit*. Anyway, I have ever since had a soft spot in my heart for cockfighters. The birds are gorgeous, and left to their own devices, fight each other. They are a reminder of braver days."

Deer opening day and the year's first real snow arrived together. The Torres family had invited us to go hunting with them, but since I have an aversion to the familial and sometimes paramilitary overtones of "drives," and in any case had a deadline, I declined. Betsy, as sociable as I am not, told me that there was no way she was going to miss the experience. Although she had never shot a deer, she loved to eat venison.

She woke me in the utter blackness of three a.m. in December to say, "It's snowing. Is that good?"

"Great. Better tracking," I mumbled, not tracking at all. She bustled about the kitchen for a few minutes, then disappeared out the front door in response to a honk as I slipped back into sleep.

When I woke properly at seven, I went to the window and stared into the white unreflective void of a total blizzard.

Later, Betsy wrote a sketch of that day. "This year I am going deer hunting with the Clan Torres, reputedly always successful in in its quest for mule deer to stock the winter larder. The Torreses number about forty in this village. They are not chic. They are what the polite term 'Spanish,' and the good ole boys call 'Mescans.' Their year revolves around deer season. Talk of hunts past pepper their July conversation, and the hunt future takes over in about the middle of September. They work well together, driving up the canyons, and have a remarkable degree of success."

"Chubby and Shirley said they would pick me up at four a.m., so I am up and singing at three, making ham and cheese sandwiches and filling the quart thermos with coffee and the merest suggestion of Jack Daniels against the cold. Looking out the kitchen window into the black winter sky, I saw snow starting, driving in almost horizontally from the east. 'Steve,' I asked, 'It's snowing. Is that good?'

" 'Snow! Yeah, help you track,' came from the dark bedroom.

" 'Good,' I said. 'It's snowing all right.'

"At four precisely a pickup swings into our driveway, and pulling on the last layer of woollies against the bitter east wind and the fine stinging snow riding it, I climbed up into the cab, mittened hands clutching the cased gun and my satchel of lunch, pockets filled with the six cartridges that for some reason I had decided was the right number. I carefully placed the 7 x 57 on the dashboard along with Chubby's 30-06 and Shirley's 303 Enfield.

"Lunch went between my feet on the floorboards. 'Did you bring something to eat?' asked Shirley. 'Ham sandwiches,' said I, 'And Oreos and apples.'

"'I brought string beans,' she said. 'It's what I had,' indicating a large sack which proved indeed to contain a huge quantity of string beans.

"We arrived at old Tomas Torres's house where many pickups were gathered in the predawn blackness. People were hurrying around. Chubby got out of the pickup, and Shirley and I moved over to accommodate Tomas, a small boy whose name I never learned, and Adolfo, Tomas's son-in-law who had a broken ankle and would neither drive nor hunt this year. Adolfo was dressed in a down jacket, jeans and tennis shoes. He was going to find out if he liked hunting, and if the answer was yes, get a license the following year.

"The snow was coming thicker and faster and we waited for everyone to get organized. Then Chubby hit the side of the truck and he and Joseph and Randy hopped in the back.

"'Won't they be cold back there?' I asked.

"'Oh no,' said Tomas, 'They've got a sleeping bag, and Joseph's half Indian. Indians don't get cold.'

"It was cozy in the cab, five people and five guns crammed in together, the heater going strong. We drove out at the head of a caravan, heading north out of town. Dawn was greying the sky. A tire went flat, and the caravan halted behind us. Everyone out except Shirley and me. We sat luxuriously, remarking that there were about twenty-five men to do the tire changing and they could jack us up perfectly easily. They did. Much beating together of hands, dusting of jackets and we were on our way again.

"'Turn here,' said Tomas, indicating a break in the cedars and a possible track under the four-inch coating of snow. We drove in, winding through the little trees till we came to a clearing. 'Here,' said Tomas. 'Stop here.'

"'Joseph,' called Shirley, 'Give Betsy your face mask. You can have her hat. You're an Indian, you don't get cold.' Joseph, small, neat, smiling, handed over the ski mask and accepted my watch cap in its place. 'I just lent it to him for the ride out,' Shirley explained to me, and I took it gratefully, for we were gathering to walk due east into the blizzard.

"Before we started, Chubby lectured us. 'Don't shoot at anything unless it's a deer right in front of you. There are people spread out on both sides. Just a deer. Right in front.' We nodded solemnly and started off, walking in line about twenty feet apart. We walked and walked into a white wall of snow, each of us a dim outline to the next. We walked slowly and carefully, as quietly as possible, into cold white needles. Where the hell are we going, I wondered, as our group, now numbering about ten, turned once again, and came out in a clearing where a blazing fire awaited and steaming cups of coffee were being handed out.

" 'Hey, nothing, we saw nothing! You see anything?'

" 'No, we saw nothing.'

" 'We put this fire out and go over to Copper Canyon,' decided Tomas, the strategist. 'We put you out at the south end and you drive up over the top. We meet you on the other side.'

"Back into the pickups we went, me carefully wiping Steve's gun free of snow and ice. And followed Tomas's directions out of the whiteness we had occupied and into another whiteness that turned out to be the road. North we drove till vague flattening indicated the left turn to Copper Canyon. As the pickup stopped, Chubby jumped out, and looking meaningfully at Shirley and me said, 'I'm going to walk up that canyon there very fast. Up over the top very fast. You want to come?'

" 'No,' said me, 'Not me, I'll stay with Tomas and see you on the other side.'

" 'No,' said Shirley, 'I'll stay with Betsy.'

"We watched the group gather, discuss who was going where, and spread out for the drive.

" 'Joseph,' I called, 'Joseph, come get the face mask. I'm staying in the pickup!' Joseph jogged over and took the mask with a smile.

"Adolfo managed to turn the pickup around in the road, and we backtracked over our rapidly disappearing tire tracks to the main dirt road, turning left and driving along for about a mile, when Tomas suddenly said, 'Turn left.'

"And then we were crossing the open range, peering through the snow at an eruption of lava rock which jolted us around as much as it is possible to jolt two men and a boy and two women jammed into the cab of a pickup. Shapes loomed up ahead, cedars, mostly. One pair of shadows said, 'Moo,' and became a whiteface cow and calf. Blood lust overcame me.

" 'I'd shoot that calf if Adolfo would stop the truck,' I muttered to Shirley. She laughed in semi-horror. 'You can't shoot a calf,' she said. 'Out here it's worse to shoot a cow than a person. They'd kill you for shooting that calf.' "

Meanwhile, I managed to shove down worry and work until about two p.m. The sky neither brightened nor darkened but simply stayed white, piling a foot and more of snow against our eastern wall. I came to know later that the rare storms that came with an east wind were the worst, and could close Sedillo Hill and shut us off from Socorro and the world for days. Right then, all I knew was that I was scared. At about three o'clock, I loaded my own heavy rifle into the little Datsun pickup and headed out of town to the north.

North of Magdalena the main road is a narrow, intermittently bad dirt track that joins the interstate after making a sixty-mile bend around Ladron peak. On it are two ranch houses, both at the point approximately halfway along where the track bogs down in the Rio Salado, a river where cow and tire tracks are more common than water. I drove carefully. Three miles along I managed to get down into and up out of La Jencia Creek, another dry river. The twenty-foot banks were scarred by tracks where spinning wheels had scraped off three inches of snow, but they were turning white even as I watched.

I managed another nine miles, out onto the flatness of La Jencia Plain. Except for that flatness I had no idea where I was. When I got out, standing back-to-the-wind so that I wasn't blinded by the gale, I could see that the only tire tracks in the world ended at my truck. The silence was broken only by the steady hiss of snow and the clanks and snaps from my cooling engine. The view resembled that on a television set when the broadcasting station has shut down for the night. I could do nothing but go home, very carefully. I backed and filled about ten times, fearful of getting a wheel in the snow and mud and then dying of exposure on the empty walk home.

And when I reached my door, a sign was stuck to it with two pushpins: "Come on down for tortillas and beer. We have two deer." When I reached the Torres house the family was posing a deer on a plastic sheet on a rug before the fireplace. As the kids crowded around the carcass and Chubby backed to the wall to get everyone into the Polaroid's frame, I toasted Betsy—and Richie and Randy, the providers—across the room. My fear and anxiety were gone, vanished like the coyote down her hole. All were present and accounted for, and our friends were gathered for the feast.

V

Big and empty, high and bright and dry.

Big and empty: when you leave Socorro the "highway," Route 60—it is really a narrow two-lane, but built for high speed traffic—runs more or less due west to Arizona, a good 130 miles; say, the length of Connecticut. Until recently, only one paved road leading out of Gila County branched from it. This road, Route 12, cuts southwest at Datil, becomes Route 180, and meanders through canyons and narrow fertile valleys to Silver City. In nearly two hundred miles it does not traverse anything bigger than a couple of villages with populations in the hundreds.

As for the rest of the pavement, Route 117 was paved through while we lived in Magdalena. It runs north from Quemado, near the Arizona border, to thread past the endless rabbit brush and eroded lava of the North Plains, squeezes between sandstone cliffs and lava *malpais*, and emerges on Interstate 40 after covering over one hundred miles. If there's a single building actually on it, it's been built this year. A paved spur runs forty miles north from Magdalena to Alamo Navajo and dies. A paved connector now links Route 60 and Route 12-180. There is a two-mile stretch of pavement running south of Magdalena, with no houses on it, for no discernible reason. Two miles of Route 70 are paved south to the very large array. And a spur of Route 52 is paved from the Rio Grande up into the Gila.

That's it. If you stack two Connecticut-sized blocks atop each other, with Albuquerque in the upper right corner of the upper block, with Magdalena on the east-west centerline, with I-40 as the upper edge and the tiny thread of New Mexico 90, which climbs over the Black Range, as the lower, these roads I have just described are the only pavement. As for towns and people, Catron county, which makes up most of the western half of this block, is also the size of Connecticut. As of 1980 it contained 2,720 people, 472 of whom lived in Reserve, the county seat.

All of this immense land is subtly or ferociously alien to anyone who has grown up in a place full of water, greenery, and people, a "normal" place with close horizons and low altitudes. When you emerge from the hills on the Magdalena side of the Plain of St. Augustine, you look down twenty-six miles of absolutely straight, virtually level highway; a perfect vanishing point as I have already said. There is nothing between you and Datil but the line of radio telescopes.

So you drive toward that point, at something like seventy or seventy-five miles per hour, thinking of the ancient lake bed as a short space to cross; left arm resting on the truck door, wind roaring, hair whipping from under the brim of your Stetson, and no thoughts to bother your head. Hawks tilt on the wind; music blasts from the tape player. It's no passage at all; just the plain, which you cross to go to the Eagle Guest Ranch to eat a steak, hurry through on the way to the real distances that lead to Davila's in Mangas, Jonay's Bar in Quemado, the county seat in Reserve. Twenty-six miles—nada.

But twenty-six miles around Boston is something else. It happened to be the exact distance between Betsy's old apartment in Newton and the house where I grew up in Easton. The idea of seeing between one and the other seems as likely as seeing from Boston to New York. Land, trees, buildings, and, as Betsy said, the very air "gets in the way." And to drive between those points is a long commute, well over forty-five minutes, more in rush hour (which now seems to stretch from seven to seven). The drive involves six or seven separate roads which lead through at least one town center and parts of four others, through either a string of traffic lights or, worse, bumper-to-bumper, stop-and-go traffic on the highway, listening to the radio and cursing.

Sometimes, when crossing the Plain at night, you will see another driver approaching. Or rather, you will see a pinpoint of light, directly ahead, seemingly unmoving. You, and he, are rushing at each other at something between fifty-five (unlikely) and one hundred miles per hour. But the light stands as steady as a star. At some distant point—still miles away, but one I have been unable to figure out how to measure—the light trembles for a moment and becomes two, side by side. Until it gets a little closer it seems as though something has happened inside your eyes.

These are high beams, of course. Even with high beams you are rarely ahead of your headlights if you are doing a comfortable seventy—you might hit a coyote, or, God forbid, a black angus could have broken a fence and be standing in your path like a dark iceberg. So, if you grew up driving in another area of the country, you begin to flick your lights down, and up, and down.

Down, up. And you wait, and those two brilliant pinholes still hover at about the same spot in front of you. Finally, you put yours down. His continue to glare into your eyes. Another minute passes. His flick low. Twenty seconds, fifteen, ten, and he dopplers past.

You hear nothing but the wind, and see nothing at all for a moment. Then vision comes back as you hum on across the inky old lake in the moonlight, with no sense of motion at all, still twenty minutes out of Magdalena.

High: New Mexico's lowest point is three thousand feet above sea level. The highest part of the state, the ridge of the Sangre de Cristos in the north, varies between 10,000 and 13,160, but 10,000-foot peaks are scattered through central and southwestern New Mexico as well, two even in the relatively tiny Magdalena range, only twenty miles from north to south.

Albuquerqueans tend to be amused, if not annoyed, by Denver's preposterous smugness at being a "mile-high city." Albuquerque, which doesn't talk about it, is 6500 feet above sea level. (Sante Fe makes 7000.) Living in a state with an average altitude of more than 5000 feet makes New Mexicans puzzled at the idea of an area where "mountains" rarely go as high as 6000 feet—in other words, the whole continent east of the Front Range. Even denizens of the intermontane plains are likely to refer in half-humorous contempt to "flatlanders," though such places as the Plains of St. Augustine or the La Jencia Plain can look awfully flat to a newly arrived New Englander.

Soon, the physical realities, the sheer difference forces itself upon the newcomer. Except for the bottoms of river courses and large arroyos, the lowest height of the plateau we came to live on is over six thousand feet. When we first arrived we noticed that if we walked a hundred yards we'd be out of breath. It was unnatural, but we were panting. We'd breathe deep, but it took a while before we felt we could go on; in a hundred feet we'd be panting again. In books we imagined that a person suffering from a change in altitude was struggling up a steep slope. But now we were walking on gritty sand, through gray, feathery rabbit brush, following Dutch Salmon's dogs over a landscape flatter than anything I had ever seen other than a salt marsh. And we couldn't breathe.

Betsy, who still smoked, was bright red in the face. (I had miraculously, with no conscious effort, quit for the road; I wouldn't start again until exile and told friends that I smoked "on the coasts.") She sat down and lit a cigarette, waving us on. And just when I thought that I couldn't continue, though idiot pride was forcing me to—idiotic because Dutch knew that it took some time to acclimate and would have gladly stopped—just when I was so winded that I couldn't speak, just then a jack started up from behind a bush at a flat-out run, all ears, black and white. The dogs accelerated like cheetahs, with such a snap of muscle and backbone that I'd swear they left smoke from burning pads. Dutch whooped and waved them on. I tried not to collapse, suspecting that my face was purple.

That night we were so tired we couldn't eat, and I had a headache. Alhough I was usually insomniac, I slept for twelve hours. In a month we could jog after the dogs. Ease at ten thousand feet took a bit longer.

In the high country, weather is vertical, hourly temperatures cut by the razor edge of shadows. Weather makes vegetation and vice versa; exposure shapes climate. Simple questions like "is it hotter in New Mexico?" (than in Boston, New York, or San Francisco) have no simple answers. Consider: in the summer, Magdalena's temperatures rarely break ninety degrees Fahrenheit. In the winter, forty degree days are common, and warm thaws of nearly seventy not rare. A mild climate, you say? Not really. More than season, "climate"—we really have no exact word—can be a result of hours, vertical feet, level miles, or mere inches from sun to shade.

Those forty degree winter days have nights that plunge into the single digits. Altitude, when all altitude is high and the air is dry, can mean differentials as harsh as those from Mexico to Canada. Socorro is in the valley and relatively humid along the river, and its summer temperatures usually top one hundred degrees. Climb ten miles to the top of the plateau and you lose ten degrees of temperature, all of the humidity, and gain a breeze. Go from there to the top of the Magdalenas four miles away and it's cool, probably in the seventies; at night, chilly. On top of the mountains frost is always a possibility.

Travel from a sunny winter day of almost fifty in Socorro onto the plateau and into its deep heart around Mangas. The total rise in elevation will be less than three thousand feet. But if it is a good, clear, still day—the kind that warms up the valley best—radiational cooling will make all the heat roar off into the star-studded void as soon as the sun goes down. By morning the temperature may have fallen to well below zero in Mangas.

As for dampness: if you go up into a slightly larger mountain range than the Magdalenas—say the San Mateos, twenty miles southwest and about twice as wide—you go up not only into cool but also toward meadows lush as an English park, often complete with grazing stags. You'll find fields of blue flag irises, little *ciénagas* or marshes, springs, and above that a Canadian profusion of fir and spruce. Big, high mountains hold the weather and wring the clouds.

The whole concept of "life zones," a vertical array of landscapes from Sonoran up through Canadian to Hudsonian (as in Hudson Bay), taught to us in bygone freshman biology courses, was born in C. Hart Merriam's brain as he looked at western mountains. It's still a useful metaphor, though as usual reality tends to be a bit more complicated. Sure, there are broad bands of like vegetation, as visible as rock strata in a stream cut. After October a straight horizontal line, white above, blue-brown below, forms on the Magdalenas. Above it, roughly at the line between the piñon-juniper and the higher, more conventionally pine-like ponderosa, the snow stays until May, forming drifts three feet deep in the sunless ravines of the northern slopes. Below it we get a snowstorm every couple of weeks, at least at Magdalena's six thousand-plus feet. But—another difference between the dry west and the flatlands—the snow vanishes until the next storm.

I didn't say "melts," though some of it certainly does. A lot of it just sublimes away, sucked back into the air by a ferocious combination of sun and dry wind. But the difference between sun and shade temperatures in high, clear places is unlike anything at sea level. At the north side of the house, where the cold, blue shade lasts all winter while the sun withdraws to the south, there is always one little patch of snow, huddled as if for safety between the adobe wall and the propane tank. It lasts for months, though the rest of the yard is brown sand and dry, brown grass. And when you stand beside it in that shade, you feel winter's chill even when, on the other side of the house, you could warm your back on sun-heated stucco and bask in fifty degrees of winter warmth. The same goes for summer. Ninety dry, skin-crisping degrees in the sun can turn into cool and comfortable beneath the Siberian elms. Is New Mexico hotter or cooler than New England?

All this jigsaw puzzle of sun and shade and altitude determines the flora. What grows where may not sound very important to those who live in well-watered climates, where everything left alone becomes first a green fuzz of weeds, then a tangled thicket, finally a forest. But here "sky determines," as New Mexican historian Ross Calvin said. Besides the life zones, vegetation differs from northern to southern exposures. Canyon sides facing south have lower altitude, more Mexican, more arid-type growth: oaks, yuccas, few large conifers. Northern-facing exposures, where the sun doesn't shine in the winter, are more Canadian; the snow builds deep and stays long, under tall poles of ponderosa pine. This pattern gives an oddly comforting sense of direction, like a biological compass.

Animal habitat is vertical too. Clarke's nutcrackers, large noisy birds like pallid crows with bold black-and-white wing flags, appear only on the highest peaks, geese and cranes only on the Rio Grande. Between are hardy species that roam everywhere like coyotes and ravens, and rarer ones that live only in specific island habitats. Red-faced warblers, tiny ground-creeping songbirds in drab gray with brilliant red-and-black hoods, live only in a narrow band of oak thickets in south-facing canyons, at about sixty-five hundred feet. Some animals even make vertical migrations. In the winter goshawks, Cooper's hawks and sharp-shins descend from the piney forests where they breed to fall on the town like avian wolves. They skulk in cottonwoods and twist and turn between the walls of Magdalena's houses exactly as they do between the tree trunks of their summer home, chasing sparrows and starlings that in turn live off the leavings of pigs and goats and fighting chickens. Nobody bothers them much, and so they are sometimes startling in their boldness; they'll stop and sit on a tree in the yard and turn to check you out, or kill a sparrow in the snow outside the window and stare up with their terrible orange-yellow cartoon eyes, as though weighing the odds of taking you down. So, in other times, must wolves have descended on winter villages.

Brightness, New Mexico's enchanted light, is the stuff of tourist brochures and coffee-table books: spotlit mountains, ruddy afterglow, white peaks above blue ranges, above warm plains the color of a mountain lion's pelt. It's almost a cliché. But it is this thin, bright air that makes it possible to see so far so clearly and therefore paradoxically think that things are smaller and closer together, like things back home in Kansas or Massachusetts. The foothills surrounding Magdalena are sprinkled with juniper. These range from eight to twenty feet high and are spaced at roughly equal distances, never clumped. When you look up from the plain you see them as separate dark heads, scattered like grains of pepper. Your eastern eyes will tell you they are bushes, knee- or waist-high, and pretty close, not trees four or five miles away.

We'd always ask visitors how far back from the road they thought Ladron's bare peak was. Westerners had little trouble. Easterners would look and say "a mile" or, if adventurous, "three or four miles." Try again. From the nearest point on Route 60 to the tip of Ladron is twenty-seven miles. We'd try to convince them.

"See that ribbon at the foot? Use the binoculars."

"Yeah, so what?"

"That's the bluffs along the Rio Grande. Look on the map. That's twenty miles in."

"I don't believe it."

If it were summer we'd never convince them, at least not down in that core where people really believe. But in winter . . .

"Okay. See those blue ridges beyond the peak, to the right a little? Two big curves? Right, there. Do they remind you of anything?"

Most wouldn't get it at first. But eventually the white upper edges, the parallel bands of subtle tints, begin to tug at memory. "They look a little like the mountains over Albuquerque. And the ones south of there when we drove down the river."

"That's what they are. The Sandias—ninety miles away. And the Manzanos, a little south."

Nothing gets in the way.

The light can be dangerous. Not in the clichéd way of old westerns, burning down to fry you in the desert like an egg on a sidewalk. Though I suppose it's possible to suffer such a fate in New Mexico, it's more likely in the low, hot and utterly arid Sonoran

Desert to the west. Rather, the light will get you in more subtle ways, if anything about New Mexico's blazing sunlight is subtle. Up this high you are less shielded from ultraviolet rays, from cosmic radiation, than down in more normal, humane habitats. You squint and get headaches and wear sunglasses and squeeze deep lines into the tissue around your eyes. Skin turns leathery early. And if you expose and burn it too much, especially if you are an Anglo, it will finally spot and turn strange and grow cancers. New Mexico has the highest rate in the nation of two odd ways to die—bubonic plague and skin cancer. It's not a place for sunbathers. Even a swarthy half-Italian like me feels a deep physical prickling and unease if I stay exposed to the sun too long, and I don't generally burn. We all may have red (or brown) necks, but we all also wear long pants and long-sleeved western shirts and, above all, broad-brimmed hats. Out here, "cowboy" clothes are a necessity, not a fad.

Last and most importantly of all, allied to and dependent on high and bright but more important to human habits and needs than either: dry.

The first signs you recognize in dry are small, for when the snow is still on the mountains, it hardly seems the Sahara. But eyes become red and prickly, even when you haven't spent all day staring into the sun. Throats are dry, even if you don't smoke. Lips are cracked and chapped. And between nosebleeds, the inside of your nose feels like it's lined with potato chips. You don't ever feel sweaty. The differences don't seem as profound as they are for a while—after all, you've got snow and a Maine-like profusion of waters above, big river swamps below. And then after a short rain, something like this happens. I quote from Betsy's account:

"Last year, as we were sitting by a cattle tank, waiting for doves to come in to the water, we heard a roaring sound behind us.

"'What's that?' I asked.

"'The water's coming,' said young Philip Mansell, laying down his gun. 'Come on, let's go see it.' And four of us ran to the top of a rise, away from the cottonwood-shaded tank. We topped it, and looked down into the sandy arroyo we had just driven across. The roaring grew, and suddenly around the bend came a miraculously perpendicular wall of water, tumbling forward, carrying behind it great boulders, small trees, odd parts of abandoned vehicles. I stood entranced as the three-foot-high wall rushed forward.

"'What's the matter?' asked Philip, looking at my astonished face. 'Doesn't the water do that in Massatooshets?'"

VI

About three years after we arrived, an earnest Midwestern friend got entangled in our perennial "should we stay or should we go" debate. He suggested we try Montana. Betsy wrote back that she and I were happier with some Spanish leavening in the culture.

He replied: "From where I stand, one hell of a long way from Mexico, there is very little about Mexican culture that I can find attractive. Machismo. The baroque religiosity. Hopelessly corrupt legal system. And everywhere the brutalizing stamp of poverty. Even the language sounds wrong in my ear—wheedling, garrulous."

I was—even apart from the maddening, false equation of Mexican and New Mexican culture that everyone northeast of Texas makes—furious. I began a reply that addressed him as "You goddamn uptight, middle-class, upper-Midwestern Protestant." But Betsy hushed me and wrote a calm letter:

"Spanish leavening. Obviously this isn't a border town, and who we speak of as Spanish are a mix of Mexican and Indian, though there are old land-grant families around too. I think it's really the visibility of an ancient culture, and an ancient religion that makes New Mexico more bearable than South Dakota.

"When I was twenty-four years old I went to Mexico to visit my aged mother who spent her winters in Taxeo where she rented a *casita* and wrote bad poetry. I went with a friend who insisted on coming along, and after we had made Mother sufficiently nervous ('They're not used to *amantes* at Los Arcos, dear'), we proceeded to Acapulco to see the sea. While there, we ran into a twenty-one-year-old woman who was engaged to the brother of a friend. When her friends went back to Mexico City, she decided to stay with us and have a fling with bullfighters and such like who found her ample charms irresistible. After a few weeks, she felt sick one day, and we left her to rest up while we went to the beach. When we came back she was worse, so we called a doctor, who pronounced her as having *turista*, and wanted her to go to the hospital. She didn't want to go, so he sent in a nurse to help care for her, and she stayed with us, and got worse and worse for four days. On the fourth day, the nurse and a sort of houseboy helped her to the bathroom and back. A nurse from Chicago was there, and next to us lived an American doctor who disapproved intensely of us all. The two Mexicans got Claire back to bed, and she suddenly turned an odd bluish color, and relaxed. Natalie from Chicago immediately started screaming 'She's dead, she's dead!' I told her to shut up. When we got back the American doctor was there as well, to yell about her immoral ways, and say this was one of the wages of sin. Claire had indeed died, the first victim of a polio epidemic. And while all this idiotic ruckus was going on, the Mexican servants and nurse gently and quietly arranged her hands, someone brought a little bunch of flowers to place in them, and someone else four candles which were lit at the four corners of her bed. No judgments, no hysterics. They moved through those screaming idiots as if they didn't exist, with dignity and sorrow, for they had liked Claire.

"There is terrible poverty in Mexico and there are terrible sleazes as well, but for the most part, I have found even the poorest people of great generosity, people who laugh a lot, people I can respect deeply.

"Here, Steve reminds me, it is the Spanish/Navajo families that ask us to their birthdays, the notorious Easter picnic, their weddings. And assume you know all their relatives. They have a kind of depth to them that I find hard to describe, and infinite kindness.

"They also beat each other up at fiestas, punctuate their sentences with *boom*, as in 'I saw the deer eight hundred yards away and shot him, *boom*.' Or, 'He came at me with a bottle, so I hit him, *boom*.' They are generally hell to be around, when they're being better than each other. But when the chips are down, they're good to know. They cook *empanadas* and *chiles rellenos* and *bizcochitos* and *posole* at Christmas. To live among ranchers without the Spanish around would be a bit grey."

Betsy had taken to calling New Mexico "a bare and bloody land," but with affection. She revelled in its grim and heroic history, in a topography that sometimes still seemed too desiccated to me. "It's like the ocean," she'd point out, as though that comparison were the most obvious in the world. "It's vast, and you have to know how to navigate. You can see the weather coming up for miles. And if you have any sense, you pack your own water. I must take you to Spain," she added. "You'd know why these people stayed here if you could see it." She found the Ted Hughes poem, "You Hated Spain," in one of my books and we quoted it aloud to each other as a gleeful charm against those elsewhere who refused to understand. "Spain frightened you. Spain / Where I felt at home. The blood-raw light, / The oiled anchovy faces, the African / Black edges to everything, frightened you. / Your schooling had somehow neglected Spain."

We had begun to relax enough to enjoy the people—Spanish, Indian, and ranch. They all raised and hunted their food, taught their children manners, kept their old people around, and buried their dead without complaint. We didn't romanticize rural life or rural people; we had spent more of our lives in the real country than we had in the suburbs. We had both been raised doing animal chores (Betsy had spent many of her younger years on a hardscrabble dairy farm in New Hampshire) and had shoveled shit, broken ice, and doctored and slaughtered before we were ten. Had we any lingering romanticism it would have been cured by circumstance; in those years our combined annual income would not exceed $12,000, and an ancient house on a remote plateau exacts its toll in colds and unpaid bills, in unrepaired machinery and teeth and animals. Still, we believed with our neighbors that our *querencia* held some parts of a real life worth living, full of good and gritty things that coastal civilization attempted to deny, ignore, or paper over. We decided, not for the first or last time, that this was the place.

We belatedly decided that we needed to reclaim our possessions and our non-canid animals, all of which were stored in Massachusetts. We had been getting by on almost nothing—a little barebones furniture from the landlady, our road "silver," three coffee cups, two skillets, a camp stove, and the one hundred books that fit under Cooper's box lid with our clothes and guns and rods and typewriter. Back east we had thousands of books, two cats, the lanner, and some real furniture, plus useful stuff like paintings and a stereo and snowshoes; in short, all the necessities of civilized life.

Our trip back was so uneventful that I remember nothing but that it took us four days, and that the sun never went behind a cloud. Our week in Massachusetts was busy but hardly social. We spent it discovering that we couldn't get all our possessions into the back of a Datsun truck.

First, we needed the books. We packed the entire bed of the truck with them until the springs nearly bottomed out and we got all but nine boxes in. We covered them with a plastic tarp, and fitted in boards over the top. Between the boards and the rickety aluminum cap, we packed everything else that would fit, mostly paintings and cooking stuff. We left the furniture; most of it still resides in Massachusetts attics. Finally, jammed in against the cap's hatch, we stuffed two carrying cases, one for the hawk and one for the cats, Audrey and Sarah. Maggie spaniel, who had come along for the ride, would make the two-thousand-mile-plus return trip sitting in Betsy's lap up front.

Our day of departure was December 28. We might have stayed longer, but the first continent-sweeping blizzard was building to the west, and even the little truck's four off-road tires didn't make us feel confident about its handling characteristics. It had never been loaded so heavily.

Hawks and dogs travel well; cats rarely do. Audrey was a sweet-natured simpleton, a vocal tortoiseshell with the thinnest coat I have ever seen on a cat. Sarah was also a tortoiseshell, a half-Persian prima donna with the personality of a rattlesnake and rather less intelligence. A veterinarian friend advised tranquilizers. Ten miles out of Boston, in the teeth of the gathering blizzard, we heard an unearthly moaning from the back. We ignored it until it turned into a crescendo of wailing, punctuated with the hisses and snarls of a serious cat fight. But there was little we could do until we reached Amherst. When we decanted the noisy box onto a friends's living room rug, Audrey bolted and hid beneath the couch. Sarah emerged more slowly, moaning and walking backwards. I reached out for her and she attacked my hand with all of the domestic cat's barely submerged wildness.

We waited out the blizzard, but it was obvious that Sarah was going to be a problem. Untranquilized, she would not get in the box and attacked Audrey as though the innocent cat were a blood enemy. Tranquilized, she walked backwards, moaned, and still attacked everything. We brought her to another vet friend, who pronounced her hopeless and then, just as we were about to despair, said that she had "always wanted a cat that looked like that." Our thanks were more than hasty—we wanted to be away before she changed her mind. Pleading the next storm as an excuse, we ran.

That storm caught up with us at the entrance to the Pennsylvania Pike. When we holed up at the nearest motel we began the unvarying routine that we were to follow for the next six nights. First, we'd bring in Audrey's box and a litter tray, and put the tray and some cat food in the bathroom. Audrey would stroll out purring with simple-minded joy, use the tray, and begin to eat. Then we'd walk Mag, and bring her in. She'd promptly tree Audrey on the commode. Finally, I'd take Gremlin, the lanner, from his dark box, give him a meal of stew beef on my fist, and return him uncomplaining to his closet. Next morning, we'd call Audrey to hers and load up. Mag would climb onto Betsy's lap and we'd roll out through the grey-white landscape until we hit another blizzard.

Later Betsy asked me what the animals must have thought of the trip.

"Mag's easy. 'We get up every morning and get in the car. We roll landscape by the windows for eight hours. I get out and poop and go in and tree the cat. We watch television and the people drink bourbon. Sleep. Then we go roll the landscape again.' "

"Okay, okay, I've got Audrey. 'They put me in a dark box and vibrate it for eight hours. I get out of the box and shit and eat and the dog trees me. Walk around and purr all night. Get in the box. They vibrate it for eight hours.' But what must Gremlin think? I don't understand birds."

"Birds are dumb. Gremlin thinks, 'Days are getting mighty short.' "

By Oklahoma City road conditions had deteriorated. We did the two hundred miles between that town and Amarillo at a crawl, locked in an endless procession of grinding eighteen-wheelers. The surface was glare ice, and even at low speed I felt that the truck's extra weight was a curse. The visibility in the icy fog was about fifty yards. We pressed on in a daze of exhaustion, afraid that two days of this would be too much to bear. At Amarillo we stopped at the surreal Big Texan restaurant for buffalo burgers and mountain oysters. But even the high-protein meal, the two shots of Jack, and the miniskirted, cowboy-booted waitress's declaration that she was from Ventura, California, but had learned her drawl to be a better waitress failed to enliven us. We wanted, suddenly, to be home.

At the next gas stop eastbound, truckers told us that the

weather was clear fifty miles down the road. As we came out of the flat Texas agricultural country, over the caprock and into the Llanos Estacados, the clouds broke up in symphonic grandeur, bars of red-gold ripping through their fabric. Below us spread the dry, dissected landscape of home. Though we were still seven hours from Magdalena, we drove to Tucumcari through beery tears of joy.

Before Betsy and I met she had kept margays, ocelots, a great Pyrenees, a standard poodle, a bobcat (in Cambridge, for eight years), raccoons, and an owl. I had raised pigeons of many breeds, flown goshawks and merlins and red-tails and an eagle, kept all manner of reptiles, bred tropical fish, and owned a Newfoundland and a Brittany spaniel. Now, as though the arrival of our dispersed animal family unlocked some long dormant impulse, we began to accumulate a menagerie. In January, we had Maggie, Luna, Riley, Gremlin, and Audrey. By June we had added forty-odd pigeons, two rattlers, and another dog, as well as a shifting series of small reptiles and arthropods that occupied a bank of terraria on the porch.

The pigeons came soon after we arrived, more or less by accident. Jim Skidmore, my Albuquerque falconry mentor, showed me two pigeons that he intended to feed to his hawks. They were bald-headed tumblers, tiny black birds with perfect white caps, and my immediate reaction to them was less humanitarian than possessive. When I was a child, I collected and traded pigeons with the maniacal acquisitiveness that other boys brought to stamps or baseball cards. "Jesus, Jim, you can't feed them out. They're too pretty."

"Cute, aren't they?" he said, unmoved. But I persisted and, amused, Jim let me take them home. It was the thin end of some kind of wedge. Within the month I had re-subscribed to the *American Pigeon Journal* for the first time in twenty years and ordered a Wisconsin breeder's entire stock of Catalonian tumblers, a flying breed that had nearly vanished in the Spanish Civil War. We installed them in an airy flight on the enclosed porch, where we could watch them, if we wished, while sitting on the toilet. This state of affairs amused or horrified our friends, depending on whether they thought "filthy" in-house birds were tolerable or not. Mike Evans, always entertained by our oddities, said that our house was more habitat than household and wrote, "The pigeons made a cooing sound like falling water that made me have to stop and piss whenever I got close." Still, however strange they seemed to friends, the loft was another unconscious concession to the idea that Magdalena was home. Pigeons are quintessential homebodies, poor companions for nomads.

One morning Betsy was on her way to the store for cigarettes when she spotted what she thought was a baby coyote in the weeds in front of the house. When she approached for a better look, it limped forward, wagging its tail. When she came back she announced, "Somebody threw away another dog." The phenomenon was painfully familiar. "On Sunday," she once told a friend, "everybody from the city takes a drive to Magdalena and throws away the dog." We had taken in six. One, a border collie, we managed to give to Tomas. The others we had sensibly and sadly fed and brought down to our vet in Socorro, to meet whatever fate awaits abandoned dogs.

"What did you do with it?"

"I put it in the back of the truck."

"Shit. Well, we need to go to Socorro anyway." I went out with water to see a perfect yellow mutt, an elegant little Spitz-type of a kind that Floyd would later refer to as a "small Indian dog" and John as "a damn rat dog." I took one look at her and, amazing myself, said aloud, "We're keeping her!"

When we drove to the Chevron station the next day, she was with us, standing on Betsy's lap, snarling at her former mates on the village streets. Rudy Lucero, who worked then at the station and was soon to become my pigeon partner, looked in and smiled. "You have the station dog. I was worried about her."

"Do you want her back?" I asked half-eagerly.

"Oh no. She isn't safe here. Two days ago an engine block fell on her after I locked her in for the night. When I took it off her in the morning she ran away. I was real worried."

An engine block? After years of witnessing Winnie's indestructibility I find it easier to believe. Since then she has carried on a war with Maggie, attacked Dobermans and sighthounds, killed snakes, eaten lizards and a moth specimen full of pins, chased deer (she weighs about ten pounds) and leaped from the window of a speeding pickup to attack the street dogs that so obviously fill her with disgust. She has survived the streets of Venice, California, and the rains of Oregon. At the time, though, I could only sigh, and name her—what else?—Winston's Chevron. She became my companion dog in a way that the mournful hounds and silly hyper spaniels never could, and surprised me by becoming the most perfect collecting naturalist's companion I could ever imagine.

Though I had been repelled by the landscape the summer be-

fore, bored by having nothing to do but look, and not seeing anything when I did look, something had shifted. Suddenly the landscape was rich and glowing, full of subtle and fascinating life.
Those baked hills held a tropical profusion of reptiles, including
such oddities as the big crevice lizards that lived on vertical walls
and were covered with bristling scales like year-old pine cones,
and bird-like collarnecks that saw you coming and ran away on
their hind legs like miniature tyrannosaurs. Four species of rattlesnake lived within a twelve-mile radius of the house. The dusty
little prairie rattler, our perennial yard snake, was the commonest
but posed little threat. In the juniper belt and in the brushy arroyos lurked—to use a loaded verb—the huge western diamondback, which Chubby called a "coontail" for its black and-white
ringed tail. It looked placid enough crawling slowly across a patch
of sand, though its five-foot length and salami-like girth might
make anyone who was nervous about snakes shudder. But if it
saw you, it would snap into a double-S coil, broad head poised an
unnerving two feet above the ground, and rattle loud enough for
you to hear it thirty yards away. And then it would often strike,
and hiss, and slide toward you, striking as it went. Diamondbacks
were the only snake that scared me, the only ones I ever killed.
Although I knew that snakes were shy and nervous and much
smaller than I was, it was hard for me not to think of diamondbacks as malevolent. Floyd was as calm about them as he was
about everything else. One day during a quail hunt he spent ten
minutes showing me a snake's striking distance by dropping cartridges on the biggest and meanest coontail I ever saw, and moving back as the snake's strikes moved it toward his legs. (He re-
trieved the shells after the snake retreated.)

Two other rattler species could easily be found near Magdalena. Betsy's favorite was the placid blacktail, a stout snake with a perfect oriental-rug pattern. It is the only rattler in which each scale is a separate color, rather than having a pattern run across the scales, giving a mosaic effect that was as pleasing up close as it was at a distance. In New Mexico blacktails are at the extreme north of their range. We found them in the dappled shade of oak canyons and, oddly, hanging around on abandoned stone wells and rockworks. Perhaps their lovely pattern evolved to camouflage them in such surroundings. They were hard to see, though fortunately so easygoing that I could barely get them to rattle. I would never have killed one, but one day picked up the carcass of the largest I had ever seen on the road north of Reserve, eighty miles down toward the Gila. Despite the ripe smell—even unfastidious Betsy banished me to the front steps—I was determined to skin it. I held my breath to keep from gagging as I scraped away layers of stinking, yellowish fat, but finally ended up with a beautiful skin, about four feet long by nine inches wide. I salted it, dried it for a week, shook it clean, painted on enough glycerin to soften it, and rolled it into a jar of glycerin and alcohol for two weeks of constant shaking and turning. At the end I had something beautiful, as soft and subtly shining as old leather. I hung it on the wall and within the hour Winnie ate the whole damn thing.

Our fourth local species was a real speciality, the banded rock rattler, which goes against every expectation you might have of a rattlesnake. It is tiny, usually less than two feet long, a pinkish tan snake with widely separated black chevrons. Rock rattlers live mostly above seven thousand feet, under bare shifting rock slides where you might think there was nothing to eat at all, where their active season could only be four or five frost-free months. I was entranced by their beauty and oddity and determined to take one home.

Then, as Betsy wrote, "I have been to Albuquerque where I bought an enormous tome on the snakes of Texas, which pretty much covers the snakes of New Mexico. The book weighs about 120 pounds and is the size of a springle spangle. The young lady in the mall book market gave me one of those young lady smiles and simpered, 'You're going to learn all about snakes and go out and look for them?'"

"'I am not,' I told her, 'I'm just going to stuff this book in my back pocket and check 'em out in the damn field.'

"But I'm very glad we got that book because now Steve knows not to even think of collecting a banded rock rattlesnake for that partially covered fish tank."

It seems that these inoffensive little snakes are the only rattler that deal in paralyzing neurotoxins rather than the tissue damaging but slower acting hemotoxins common in pit vipers. This means, in practical terms, that a bite can stop your breathing in a half an hour. What's worse—or, maybe, funnier—is that all but one of the recorded victims have been herpetologists and collectors. Reluctantly, I put aside that idea.

Still, the house had begun to fill up with odd congeners. As Betsy said, "It's nice to have insects and small creatures to hunt when the proper seasons are over." I hadn't done "summer hunting" since I was about twelve; in the East there was always another stream to fish. Here, we rediscovered the glorious diversity of creatures available to full-time hunter-gatherers. Winnie combed the field ahead of me, barking whenever she spied a lizard or snake, digging out small mammal burrows, attempting to demolish pack rat nests. She, unlike the more domesticated dogs, had strong instincts as to what was dangerous; she'd hang back ten feet from a diamondback, barking hysterically, poke deftly at the little brown scorpions she disclosed for me under the oaks, and retrieve lizards only slightly punctured. She treed turkeys, and gobbled beetle grubs like a fox.

I took up serious insect collecting, bought nets and several sizes of pins and display boxes, killing and relaxing bottles, a spreading board and several identification keys. One of the most amazing things I have ever seen was the instant transformation of everyone I knew into a maniacal bug hunter. Betsy, of course, but also Becky and John Davila, Chubby and Shirley, Dan from the Forest Service, Rudy Lucero and his eight-year-old son Miguel, biologist Charles Galt, and Floyd all began to bring me specimens. So many came in that I could not keep up with the flood, but filled my freezer with jars of specimens waiting to be processed.

The Davilas concentrated on the brilliant, long-horned boring beetles that they found in the logs and sawdust piles generated by their wood business. The kids, Floyd's grandson and Miguel, brought me every common specimen in the village. Rudy, though, was the most dedicated and the most scientific. He came in from the gas station one day with an incredible insect, a huge grasshopper with camo-pattern wings and an armored crest arching up over its thorax.

"My God, I don't have any idea what that is. Where'd you get it?"

"I thought you'd like it. It's a little squashed. But maybe you can straighten it out in your jar. I got it out of the grill of a car."

"Local?"

"No, he was just passing through. But I know you like to write down where you get them, so I asked him where he was heading from. He just drove up from Cruces." And, when I keyed the little dragon out, I found that it was a great crested grasshopper, *Tro-pidolophus formosus*, and that its habitat was indeed the low Chihuahuan desert grassland around Las Cruces.

Betsy provided the most excitement. I am severely allergic to all hymenoptera—wasp, bee, hornet—stings, and must carry a hypodermic pre-loaded with epinephrine with me in the warm months. We had all the normal stingers here, plus some specialties. The finest, and scariest, was the Tarantula hawk, *Pepsis formosa*, a magnificent black and orange wasp as large as a hummingbird that hunts like a falcon and looks as though it would clank as it walked. I coveted one, but was glad to let Charlie Galt collect it for me. I feared it more than I feared diamondbacks; snakes don't fly. We also had a beautiful example of the principal of mimicry, a thing called a Midas fly. These harmless insects looked, and flew, exactly like the deadly wasps. I was always chasing them, but they were alert and swift and I could never surprise one. One morning Betsy came in from the post office with a humming envelope. "I've got your Midas."

"How?" I asked, feeling a little professionally jealous.

"It was buzzing in circles on the driveway in front of the post office." She ripped open the envelope and decanted it onto my book.

I did a record backwards sitting high jump.

"*Jesus Christ Bets, that's a Pepsis!*" We got it in the killing jar somehow, wondering why it couldn't fly. Three hours later, sure it was dead, we dumped it out and found that another aerial predator had neatly decapitated it, which, of course, had barely slowed it down. Annie Dillard has the word on bugs: "fish gotta swim, birds gotta fly; insects, it seems, must do all manner of horrible things."

But a lot of the summer fauna came to us. House lizards, a

constant in most sunny rural climates, were new to me. Pancake-shaped horned "toads," racerunners quick as guilty thoughts, dull little earless lizards with shaded chevrons on their sides, all sprang from the yard's soil. But fence lizards, pert saw-scaled critters with at least the presence of a parakeet, moved right inside. They would watch you from black eyes as bright as chips of volcanic rock and bob up and down when they met, flashing iridescent blue patches at each other like badges. The cat Audrey stalked them as practically as she, and all cats, did all prey. Crouch, wiggle, gnash, run, pounce, shake: dead. And dropped; a motionless lizard lacked any appeal. They lay with their sad white bellies pointed up until we found them with our bare feet, or Mag picked them up.

Mag's lizard hunting was more obsessive, and odder. Every morning when we let her out she would race around the concrete perimeter of the dog yard, freezing in an un-spaniel-like point if she saw a lizard. The two of them would both hold, still as photographs. Then Mag would pop into the air and come down with her head between her paws, to raise it juggling a wet mouthful of lizard. She had no desire to kill them, just to "object-carry." But the lizard would drown if we didn't get it away fast. Mag could carry them, live or dead, for hours; the only things she liked to carry more were white-out bottles and matchbooks.

The arthropod contingent was tropical in its profusion. As the heat gathered we were invaded by successive waves: moths first, which piled up in the light fixtures, then fragile ant lions with four paddle-shaped wings, that Chubby called "night dragons." Just before the rains came the hated black bugs. They were the only insects that acted cautious, slinking between their hiding places as if they knew we loathed them. I never could get a good specimen, because I inevitably collected them by throwing whatever I was reading at them as hard as I could.

With the insects comes legions of predators: spiders, hundreds of centipedes, and solpugids. I didn't mind the spiders, and I enjoyed the solpugids. These weird spider relatives only came out late at night. They had huge jaws, no visible eyes, and moved like mechanical toys in precise stops and starts. Sooner or later they'd encounter a moth or a black bug and bear it off to devour it under the couch like a tiny retriever.

The centipedes gave me the creeps. The little ones were bad enough, but once when John heard me complain about them he said, "You ever see a real big one?"

"And never hope to."

"They're big, man. Almost a foot long. I had one fall on me once and it felt like a metal chain. Kinda heavy, and cold-like."

I shuddered. And of course, a week later, I opened the door to let Winnie out in the dark and felt something fall to my neck. It was heavy, and cold, and moving. I clawed for the light, yelling, and was not surprised to see a nine-inch reddish horror squirming off across the floor. There was no way I was going to step on it with bare feet. I wore shoes everywhere outside of bed for a week.

As usual, the dry heat of the early summer made me restless, even with all these good distractions. I had begun my first book and could not settle down to it. A New York publisher's encouraging letter came in, together with an invitation to one of my six sisters' wedding. We decided to fly to Boston, then down to New York, to see what kind of a deal I could make.

That week blurs in retrospect; it was, really, not just implausible but impossible. Within twenty-four hours we attended my sister's wedding and sold my first book. But the third incident in that day could not have occurred in fiction: Virginia, in health and joking the morning of the wedding, died. She had always complained to us, more officiously than plaintively: "What shall you do if I die while you're in New Mexico?" Betsy had told her that, most likely, we'd attend her funeral. Now she had gone and done it at ninety-four, while we were home, and there was one part of me that had to applaud her always perfect timing. Or as Betsy said, grinning past an obligatory tear, "What good judgment Mother showed in waiting for us to be here."

Still, it was more than just crazy: dancing and talking and drinking all night at the wedding, arriving at Betsy's sister Jane's where we were staying at 8 a.m. only to be told that Virginia had slipped into a coma, her death that afternoon, a drive to New York to make the deal over dinner and drinks, then a burnt-out drive back to plan the funeral. During all of it people kept asking why we lived in New Mexico. Through it all, I kept wondering why we weren't there.

The worst part was not the muggy heat, or the inevitable stress attendant to weddings, funerals, and book sales. It was that, for the first time since we had moved, we were exposed to people other than our closest friends, people who asked dumb questions about New Mexico or thought they hated it. "How can you stand the heat?" "How can you stand having no trees?" "How can you live in a state with no bookstores?" (Restaurants, night life, ocean, old friends, family . . .) "Aren't you afraid to live in such an isolated place?" "What do you do all day?" "How can you stand the people?" (This last questioner was sure that we would be killed by some unholy cowboy/Baptist/NRA/Ku Klux Klan bigot; I debated telling him I had been an NRA member since 1969.) "I couldn't live in the desert." "I saw on the news that Phoenix is 106 degrees today. Don't tell me that's not hot!" And worse, the kind of New Englander who "knew" New Mexico: "How close are you to Santa Fe?" (Taos, Ghost Ranch . . .) "Right, Georgia O'Keeffe." "I love Santa Fe. It's so spiritual!"

I kept repeating, over and over: "We're at 6500 feet; it's cold at night; we have no saguaro cactus, but we do have hundred-foot pine trees, blue spruce, and trout streams; two hours south of Albuquerque, cold at night, higher than your (watch that pronoun) 'mountains'; cold at night; October snow; mountains. I like ranchers; old Spanish culture; guns; chase things with dogs and hawks; spiritual as any town with houses in the high six figures and no native inhabitants; cold at night; cooler than here; *not hot*; Phoenix is two hundred miles away and five thousand feet lower and *in another state!*" Betsy just laughed. It seemed that, for the first time in my life, I had become a local patriot.

We flew back into a black wall of thunderheads. They began to shake our plane like a dog shakes a rat as soon as we crossed the Sandias to begin our approach to the Albuquerque airport. By the time we started our drive south we were driving through solid icy waterfalls of rain, so hard and thick that we had to pull over and let them pass before we could see to go on. When we topped out on the plateau the sky had cleared and the air was full of the pungent smell of wet rabbitbrush. Nighthawks wobbled on columns of air, beeping like cartoon characters. In the yard the blue of the lilacs and the creamy white of yucca spikes stood out against the green of the hedge. They never bloomed at the same time again.

VII

"Marry me?"

"Oh, love, I'm so old. Besides, look at Mary. Do you want to end up taking care of an old crazy lady?"

"For you, it would be a pleasure."

"Don't be so romantic. It would be hell. But thank you, love."

Betsy's sister Mary had been on our minds since Virginia's funeral. Once she had been a ferocious radical, later a country housewife. She and Betsy were not close, and I hadn't met her until the funeral, where she shocked me by staring at her father's grave, then asking me whose it was and when he had died. In the intervening months it had become obvious that she had Alzheimer's or something similar. Betsy was not one to talk about her worries, but I could see that she was bothered by more than just sisterly compassion. Before, we had no money, but no debts either. We carelessly spent whatever came in, on guns, clothes, books, exotic food, or whatever took our fancy. Now there was an undertone of worry. "What would happen to me if you died?" she asked me one day.

"I don't know what you mean."

"If you died and we had no income, I'd become a crazy old bag lady. Imagine Mary without Pete."

"Love, you're part of an Italian family now. They'd take care of you. You think my father would let you starve? He'd probably give you a job!"

"That'll be okay till he gets old. Your grandmother is as crazy as Mary."

The subject disturbed me, because I had never watched her worry before. She'd shake it off for a month, then come up with things like, "I'm so old, Stephen. All my friends are dead."

Still, we never got sensible about finances. About that time, Betsy's former husband died in a car wreck. She had walked away from his increasing alcoholic instability and rage years before, without asking for a cent. Now we found he had kept up one insurance policy in her name. She inherited what was for us an enormous sum, all of $2500.

"What will we do with it? The car needs a valve job. . . ."

"The hell it does. This is yours. What do you want to do with it?"

"I guess I'll just have to get a horse."

It was the obvious choice. Like many women of her background she had grown up on horseback. Until we came to New Mexico she had ridden twice a week. Other priorities had taken up our time, and she hadn't been on a horse for several years. She had missed it. Though she never complained, she spent a lot of time just watching horses, and telling stories about her riding days. Now she began to comb the classifieds and call people up and down the Rio valley who had horses for sale.

Her taste in horses remained eastern. She wanted something tall, with thoroughbred blood, rather than the ubiquitous quarter horses and cold-blood cow ponies. Finally she found a sixteen-hand mare in Albuquerque that seemed perfect. But after riding her around the corral with a born horsewoman's ease, she shook her head quietly to me and told the owners she wasn't sure.

We left. "What was the matter with her?"

"Not her, love. Me. I've never been so out of condition in my life. My legs are shaking. I can't even evaluate a horse when I feel like this. I'm going to have to ride twelve hours a week for at least a month before I can even pick one out."

She began her regime in a valley stable north of Socorro. For two weeks she was in a state of high excitement as her dormant skills and reflexes returned. And then a bee spooked the nervy little Arab gelding she was riding into a flat-out bolt. She was later to say that if she had been in shape she would have turned him, and if she had been totally out of shape she would have fallen before he got going. Instead she hung on for fifty yards and hit the ground hard.

I had been doing laundry. When I drove in to pick her up, she was nowhere in sight. When the owner came out saying, "Don't worry," I knew we had trouble. She sat on a bench in the yard smoking. Her face was gray and set. "I'm fine," she said with an uncharacteristic brusqueness. "Just a little winded."

I was more frightened than angry, but as one does in these situations, snapped. "You might put out the fucking cigarette." She flipped it at my feet and attempted to stand as swiftly but winced and sagged. "I think I bruised my chest."

On the way to the hospital—she wanted to go home, but I had turned against our usual pattern of "no complain, no mother" and insisted—she smoked three more. They x-rayed her immediately and called our doctor and friend Bob Markwell. Bob was a bearded Kansan, younger than I, perpetually boyish. He brought the plates over to where we sat on a bench. "Shit, Bets, you really did it. Look at the ribs: one, two, three, four, five. And I think the lung's collapsed too." The breaks looked like a jagged lightning strike.

Though she refused to be kept down, one night's attempted breathing in Magdalena showed her that the doctors were right. She could not sleep at more than 6500 feet without oxygen, and her scarred lung needed it a little even at Socorro's 4500. So we moved into a motel, and I learned, for the first time, how to work an oxygen tank.

She fought off the constraints as soon as possible. Four weeks later we attended a Torres wedding where Uncle Benny, an enormous bearded man who is a part-time *curandero*, attempted to show us how to cure her pain by a kind of cupping: "You put the candle under the cup, lit. It sucks up the air and then it sucks up the meat. When it sucks up you move it *around* and *around* and *around*." He suited his actions to the words, massaging Betsy's aching ribs in a powerful circle as he belched vodka fumes in my face. I backed off, alarmed for her ribs and choking on the alcohol smell, only to have him release her and roar in a voice that could be heard at the top of the mountain, "Don't worry, Stevie, I ain't going to feel your wife's titties!"

In spite of such treatments she prevailed, but something curious happened: she lost a lot of the strength in her opposite leg. It just didn't last anymore. In a bout of desperation she took it to Socorro's Chinese-Venezuelan acupuncturist, Simone. But though she could report a flush of warmth to the leg, it remained weak, even a year later.

Since the money we had hoped to spend on the horse had to go to the ribs, she began to hatch new money-making schemes. Her good humor returned, fed perhaps by even a few weeks on horseback. That little time had reminded her that she needed to ride, as I needed to hunt, and she was determined to make enough to buy us both some live transportation.

Her first efforts were in photography, which she had done semiprofessionally before. Her first project was the jacket photo for my book. She took about six rolls of me with Gremlin: both of us in front of the old adobe, framed with chile *ristras*; me in the yard, with the Magdalenas behind; me by the lilac-yucca hedge. But none of them seemed to satisfy the publishers. Margo at the New York office kept pointing out the stuff in the background: old houses, older cars, wires, farm machinery, and worse. "You want to show them how beautiful and wild and free the West is," she'd say.

"Why don't we just tell her the West is beautiful, but not pretty," grumbled Betsy. "She wants a damned calendar." Finally Margo sent us a sketch of her concept: noble falconer, bird on fist, against the sky. Bets pondered it awhile ("there's no background that pristine within ten miles"), then hit on an idea. She had me stand on a junked Coca-Cola cooler we had stored in the yard for three years, intending to turn it into a smoker. She got down in the dirt, wincing at the pain in her ribs, and shot me from below. This time the first roll of film passed muster.

She also considered writing a book. Her first idea ("I'm a hack by trade") was to do a romance novel. Everyone said they were easy and lucrative. Her only trouble was that she had never read one; her firm tastes ran to Sybille Bedford, Anthony Burgess, Patrick Leigh Fermor, and classic travel writing. She attacked the subject like a scientist, going to the Socorro library and returning with twenty paperbacks, which she read in two days. "It's simple," she announced at the end of her research. "You have to set up the heroine in an exotic setting, then do something to the plot at page 111, then again at 160. There have to be two men; the unsuitable wild one is the one who wins the heroine's heart. I can write it in a week. I'm going to put all our friends in it."

And she did. When she finished and brought it to me I was not so sure. *The Cry of His Hounds* featured a hero based on Dutch Salmon, an impossibly naive WASP heroine of Betsy's background, an obvious John Davila, and lots of hound lore and New Mexico scenery. The trouble was, it was hilarious.

"You can't do that, Bets. The people who read these don't have any sense of humor."

"Nonsense. I have been perfectly solemn. The girl is an idiot, just as she should be." She was furious. I couldn't argue with her, partially because I hadn't done the research. But there was a bigger reason, one I never told her. In the second chapter, Amanda Brigham meets a couple from Boston who settled in the backcountry town twenty years before, who have transformed a "blue adobe brick" into an elegant southwestern house, who raise coursing dogs, who write and do sculpture. The woman is "elderly," the man gray-haired and middle aged. "Caroline" almost shyly tells Amanda that moving to the Southwest was "the second best thing that happened in my life; the first was meeting Tom." It was something Betsy would not have said aloud, nor would she, always the fatalist, ever have spoken of such idyllic hopes. She sent the manuscript off, got a prompt rejection letter, and never mentioned it again except to say, "You were right. Those people are even dumber than I thought." In the intervening years I forgot Caroline and Tom, until now.

The next project was one that she had doubts about. Nick Lyons, publisher of my falcon book and one of the last old-fashioned editors in New York, had heard our tales of Betsy's China childhood and of the Mitfordian politics of her family. "Why don't you consider some sort of autobiography?" he had asked her.

Betsy dismissed the idea at first. "If you look under the surface, my family is mundane. Only one person in each generation has any brains at all. The rest are the nicest, dullest people on earth." After the collapse of the Great Romance Novel, I began to nag her about her book.

"C'mon, Bets. You do that one and you'll be the famous writer, not me. Your family are wonderful characters. Tell 'em about wearing red to repel demons, or how your father grabbed the bandit's pigtail on his first trip up the Yangtze, or Socialist Roads, or . . ." At first she dismissed the idea out of hand but finally, sighing, sat down at the typewriter to spend a week smoking and mumbling and cursing and sometimes even hitting a key. At the end of that time she showed me seven pages headed with the enigmatic title, *China Plan*.

She began: "Once I knew a charm to bring a snail out of its shell, but it was in a language I no longer know in a country I shall never live in again. The last time I used it I was sitting on a flattish rock under a massive beech tree with my dearest friend, another five-year-old, named Bao-Bao for his resemblance to a steamed dumpling. To him I was Han Mei-Mei, daughter of the house where his father worked. The snail was between us, and we bent forward, murmuring the magic words. Promptly the little horned head poked out of the shell, and we cried out in admiration at the power of the charm."

The seven pages were full of haunting detail and personal revelation: "Honor from my mother was usually earned by doing something difficult or unpleasant. Either way it was something of a bore, since if it were difficult and pleasant one enjoyed doing it, and being honored for it was superfluous, and a simple thank you was enough for doing something you didn't want to do." There were fishing cormorants and plough buffaloes ("I always wanted one"), punkah coolies and candlelit Christmas trees. And there was an unalterable otherness that comes from being raised in a very different time and place, perhaps one that had made her a perpetual traveler: "But in my heart of hearts I shall always know—even as I find it impossible to have my ears pierced because I can feel the bandits ripping the earrings out—that the bridge of my nose is too high. Whenever a conversation turned upon noses (and thank God this was an unusual occurrence) I felt like climbing on my tricycle and riding rapidly out of sight, shame and rage surging against the knowledge that losing my temper, raising my voice, would result in an irremediable loss of face."

"You see? Mundane! Just the daily lives of some very ordinary people." She was immovable, and would have burned the whole production—she had notes as well, which she refused to let me see—but for my insistence that she put the pages away "in case you feel better about it later." Again, I found them when I started this book—thirty-four pages of narrative, not "notes," all as good as the first seven.

"I need some jobs," she declared, and went out looking. She had worked in publicity before, and was good at self-advertisement; soon she had three. "In Magdalena you either have three jobs or none," she wrote to our friends the Grooms. "I now have three, and all three together do not add up to a living. One: I am the reporter for Magdalena and points west for the Socorro

Defensor Chieftain. Two: Once a month I deliver the Magdalena *Mountain Mail*, make a deposit of the funds thus garnered, and send happy news to Iceland (the publisher has a temporary job there). And three: The village Board of Trustees has hired me to write a monthly summary of its doings in hopes of getting the townspeople involved more. I think it's quite hopeless, but am perfectly willing to take their money."

The reporting job gave her, and us, the keys to the country we hadn't had. Her beat was all of western Socorro and Catron counties, an area larger than Connecticut with five paved roads and fewer than three thousand people. She made her money on mileage, covering rodeos and Bureau of Land Mangement meetings and fiestas. And she discovered cow culture, where despite her tweed jacket and exotic accent, she found herself at home.

At first she was amused, especially by rodeos. "I plowed through two-foot-deep mud, fighting for footing among large, fancily dressed equines, up a ladder into the judges' box. 'I need a picture of the Queen,' said I. 'We don't have a Queen,' said Linda Saulsberry, wife of Leburt Saulsberry, and daughter of Buddy Major who sponsors the rodeo. This left me feeling a bit deflated. I mean, I had been specifically instructed to get a picture of the Queen. So I took many pictures of people falling off Brahma bulls (that's pronounced 'Braymah,' in case you don't know) and rising from the mud under the hooves of saddle broncs, struggling heroically with maniacal calves, landing on their heads in semi-liquid mud after parting company with bareback broncs, I learning in the meantime, because the judges' box is reached by an overpass spanning the stock area, that bareback horses are ridden with a little leather half-saddle with a hand grip built into it and aren't bareback at all." Betsy also went to fairs: "The Catron

County Fair: a four-day celebration of meat in the form of cattle, sheep, pigs, rabbits, and chickens raised by 4-H children and auctioned off at gloriously inflated prices, interspersed with the inevitable rodeo (see winners' lists in the *Defensor Chieftain*), a horse show (see also winners' lists—at this point wish I were paid by the inch), and a judging of same animals to be sold (see Betsy crawling around on her belly like a reptile in a deep bed of sawdust and variegated shit, camera in right hand, list of beasts in other, noting down what picture of whom)."

Soon, though, she became a hard-core fan, able to point out all the fine points that I missed. I liked watching the real cowboys well enough, but usually would go along for the ride and end up sitting in the pickup, reading or making notes, during the interminable children's events. Often the Davilas would join us. Beck would watch John and Betsy in animated discussion about what some fool groaning in the dust had just done wrong, and grin knowingly.

"Two of a kind."

"Mmm?"

"They're two of kind. Horseback aristocrats. And they don't have one nickel between them."

It wasn't all ranch stuff, though. Betsy joined the fire department to get their news, and beeper, and learned how to fill Scott Air Packs and fight fires. She covered a gunbattle and a small riot (both in progress) and a grisly Navajo murder trial and an even uglier air crash. She still drew the line at some subjects. Taking photos of trophy elk or mule-deer bucks was fine. But one day we were heading down to Socorro when we saw the largest diamondback rattler of our lives, five feet long, wiggling desperately across the road. We coasted to a stop, Betsy clutching her camera, me my snake stick. I wanted to show the monster to Floyd, and figured I could put it in the empty back of the truck. But before we could get to it, a huge four-wheel-drive truck skidded to a stop across it, then backed up for another run.

We left in disgust. Three hours later a smiling cowboy knocked on our door, holding up the carcass. "I understand you're the lady from the paper. I was wondering . . ."

"I don't do rattlers," she said firmly, and shut the door in his face.

VIII

We settled into our routines. The years blur together in the middle eighties. I can tell you that we still couldn't afford to buy a horse, that I started two new books, that we discovered new pleasures—catfishing, fossil hunting, flying falcons on the table-flat plains of eastern New Mexico. Though we never made the conscious decision that this would be our home forever and ever, we were less restless.

Things began to have specific places and times, in the house and yard and mountains, in the days and seasons and years. Evenings we'd sit on the landlady's sprung couch in the living room, reading. A friend had given us a Cape buffalo skull from Zimbabwe that measured three feet from horn tip to horn tip; having no place else to put it, we placed it on the coffee table. Each curved black horn encircled a pile of current reading, Betsy's on the left, mine on the right. The heavy boss where the horns met provided a stable platform for coffee cups; the slightly chewed nose bones now housed a broken mousetrap to warn away Maggie, who had done the chewing. Television and stereo and phone were near if we wanted those diversions after a day of using our brains; if they were on, they would be turned up loud so that whoever was cooking that night, around the corner in the kitchen, could hear too. Two or three dogs would encircle our feet, while Luna and Mag or Winnie would hold out to sit between us on the couch. If it were winter, a tattered afghan and a down sleeping bag in even worse condition would be wrapped in there too. It was our kingdom, and we were content. I can still see Betsy suddenly grinning up at me for no reason. "What?" I asked. "Nothing. I'm just so fond of you."

By spring each year we would be impatient to top out on the high ridges, to get up above ten thousand feet where the horizon was a hundred miles away. I'd inevitably start too early in the season. I'd park the truck at the dirt cattle tank at the bottom of Hop Canyon and start up through mud and oaks and cow tracks and newly green meadows, past mazes of gopher earthworks exposed by the melting snow, past bear diggings and turkey droppings, breathing deeply and inhaling spring's new wet air. Soon I'd be panting; there's no exercise in deep winter that compares with climbing three thousand feet in a couple of miles. Winnie would race ahead yapping like a mad fox, spring around, attack the snow, dig, bark at an imaginary quarry at the bottom of the new hole, pounce, fling herself backwards, and race off again. As we began to climb the steeper switchbacks through Douglas fir and Ponderosa on the canyon's west wall, we'd start to encounter real snow, two feet deep and clinging. Finally the trail would turn into black bogs separating stretches of hard-crusted snow deeper than my waist. In the sunny stretches hummingbirds would materialize in front of my face with a twitter of wings, hang whirring for a long second, then buzz away too fast for my eyes to follow. I'd sweat, soaked to the skin, a likely candidate for hypothermia, while Winnie would still be charging up the trail, skimming over the snow's crust, trotting daintily around the mud-holes, snorting the scent out of deer tracks, and moaning with annoyance every time I stopped and raised my binoculars.

After two or three such excursions I'd manage to get past the last nearly vertical meadows under the ridge, all the way to the top. Now Betsy would join us, in her own way. She had always been a leisurely climber, and claimed that her smoke stops revealed more wildlife than I ever saw. Now, with her bad leg, she might drop an hour or more behind me. If I waited at all obviously she would be furious. She'd walk slowly up, taking pains to stroll rather than labor, only her reddened face betraying her effort. She'd stop and eye me angrily from under her bangs as she lit a Camel. "Do not wait for me. I am not an invalid. If you insist on seeing me as a burden I shall not come." I was reminded of the time she had told me about some boyfriend who said that he "needed" her. "I told him that I didn't want to be a necessity or a responsibility. I prefer to be an irresistible luxury." I learned to go ahead at my own pace, to wait without worrying in the soft meadows of the high saddle. I'd spread lunch there amidst blue flag irises and tiger swallowtails, pop the cork on the wine, throw sticks for the dog, and smile when she said, after ambling across the flats with her hands in her pockets, "I like this terrain better."

My own temper would usually snap at the end of any long day in which I couldn't get writing done. I'd drink too much, get scared about our endless poverty, gnaw my worries like a bone, and snap at foes real and imagined. Finally I'd flee the house and drive through town, then up the long series of hills to the west until I reached the highest. If it were still light I could see the Plain of St. Augustine, an always-tranquil sea, to the west. I'd turn and park and let the wind blow through the car. When I was calm I'd drive the ten miles down to the town as fast as I could. Magdalena would start as an insignificant cluster of white specks or a line of yellow lights, spanning less than my thumb's width at the foot of the hills, then spread across the horizon until man's works replaced rock and juniper. I'd gear down at the arroyo bridge and drive through town at a sedate thirty-five. When I came back in, a little sheepish, Betsy would hand me a fresh Jack Daniels. She would say no more to me about my flight than I would have said about her slow climb to the ridge.

We learned the times of the low country, too. Before dawn in the Bosque del Apache everything would be gray. We'd go there in December for the geese, not the huge dark Canadian honkers of back east but the smaller, white and ink-black snow geese. They wintered along the Rio Grande in the tens of thousands, and as soon as the sun rose we could see hundreds at once. Their musical clanging would rise and fall like the wind, sometimes resolving into individual yips like distant beagles or, well, lone geese, sometimes pierced by the rolling, stuttering trumpet bleats of the cranes. Against the thunderstorm-colored bulk of the Magdalena foothills to the west we'd see swerves and eddies of geese, not "vees" but flurries, storms, blizzards, trading north and south as far as the eye could see. At the same time smaller parties of cranes would land in the next field, their approaches endless, almost excruciating. A crane would seem to hang motionless in the air for seconds, minutes, legs dangling, before it would stall and fold. Sometimes you'd see a flock of blackbirds erupt from a hedge to join the commuter herd in the sky. It would change shape: a bee swarm, a spirit, a blowing cloud, wind on flat water. It would squeeze into a ball and rise like a balloon as a sharp-shinned hawk cut up from below. The swarm would divide, the hawk pass through without touching either half, the hawk fall to the trees below. Then the swarm would re-form and blow like smoke downwind to the east.

And there, from the east: a little party of snows, six, no seven birds, head-on, honking. Floyd and I crouched and hid our faces automatically. ("Betsy, get your face down quick.") When the whisk of their wings seemed just overhead and the waiting past unbearable, we stood and pointed and fired. I got one over the barrels of my ten-bore and then lost it momentarily in the boom and recoil, hearing the bang-ratchety-bang of Floyd's pump and the whirring of Betsy's camera. Three birds fell, one still braking, wings ruffling and two straight down, to land with a startling grain-sack thump on the bank in front of us. All three were dead, but I held the bead on mine for a long moment as it subsided like a deflating balloon. Betsy broke the moment's solemn hush. "What did those Californians name their geese?" I must have looked blank. "You know—Easter, Thanksgiving, Deirdre's birthday? Well, I think we just shot Christmas."

At dusk in the Bosque, the concentrating hordes of roosting birds can give the modern watcher a ghostly illusion of Pleisto-cene plenty. Thirty thousand wings can drown man-made noises like the winds of a hurricane, and the chorus of voices is no less innocent. We'd see whooping cranes here and there amidst the legions of gray sandhills, white and as tall as men. There might be a bald eagle sitting on the ice, squat and stolid as a tree stump, crammed with scavenged meat and unwilling to move away from the insect attacks or crows or marsh hawks. If we drove around the perimeter one of those marsh hawks would be likely to use our vehicle as a flush dog, dipping and weaving ahead of us in the twilight, a dark V with a white band across its rump like a tail-light. Or we might see a coyote trotting home with an enormous white goose hanging from its mouth, proud and crafty as a character in a folktale. Or a ponderous great blue heron, a mule-deer buck with his head high in alarm, a glossy black-necked pheasant. Once, just once, we saw a band of white pelicans, marked like the snow geese but as huge and solemn and prehistoric as pterodactyls. As we watched they rose up on the day's last thermals, flapping and soaring like hawks, until they disappeared into the pink, unclouded sky.

More dusks, more dawns, different seasons. At dusk on the river in June, when we'd fish for channel cats and flatheads and yellow bass on the man-made ground between the river and the ditches where the village of San Marcial stood until a flood erased it in the thirties. It's a no-man's-land there, flat and low, overrun by the feathery alien growth of tamarisk. The desert looms up above. The only solid ground is the ditchbank which runs with geometrical precision into vanishing points as sharp as those of the roads on the plains. As we'd drive in through the maze of changing, flood-altered roads, little groups of half-wild black cattle would appear and disappear in the salt-cedar thickets. It would be hot and sticky and smell like dead fish and water and orange blossoms all mixed together. When a fitful breeze passed, the leaves on the great cottonwoods that still towered over the salt cedar would rattle and turn over to show their white undersides. We'd throw in our lines, anchor our rods, and watch for new things. As the dusk deepened, herons would fly up the river and a chorus of birds, amphibians, and insects would combine to make the river sound like a grade-B jungle movie. We'd sit by a Coleman lantern and swat mosquitoes, sip whiskey and tell stories, and wait for whatever might bend our lines. We knew there were monsters out there.

Or dawn in town, the day of a *matanza*, literally a "killing," a Torres family pig barbecue. Once Betsy rose early, before sunup, for the actual death, wanting to document the whole process for a project she called the Matanza Cookbook. While Chubby had warned her that the process could be gory, she faced it determinedly. When I arrived I asked her how it had gone down. She said: "Very smoothly. They use a .22, but they know where to shoot it. The pig fell in its tracks like it had never been alive. The only thing that bothered me was how the other pigs watch."

By the time we usually got there the pig had lost its identity. The Torres men had gutted it, draped it in steaming burlap, beheaded it, and scraped off its hair. They'd saw the meat into various cuts while sweating and drinking beer. Uncle Benny would cut the *chicharrones*, the cracklings, into long strips and then into chunks. The women would already have collected the blood and cooked it into a sort of loose hamburger consistency, either hot with chiles or sweet, with raisins. I'd roll some into a tortilla, grab a beer, and volunteer for the one job I knew well, stirring chicharrones. For the next hour I'd paddle the hissing chunks around with a stick or a crowbar in their container, a lengthwise half of a fifty-gallon drum suspended over a pit of burning piñon logs. It was thirsty, two-handed, muscular work, a good excuse for morning beer and flour tortillas full of organ meats and green chiles. I believed I was good at it; anyway, I never burned anything.

In 1985 the editor of the Albuquerque *Journal*'s weekly magazine, *Impact*, asked me to do an article on what it was like to be a Bostonian in Magdalena. I did a light, rambling piece, taking off from the old "Why I Live Where I Live" series in *Esquire*. I talked about my friends, food, hunting, cockfighting, weather, even our ambivalence. I cited an old cowboy from a book on working cowboys: "It's hard to see what a man would like about this part of the country. It is hot, dry, and dusty in the summer, cold, dry and dustier in the winter. I left it twice, but both places I went were worse."

I made two mistakes. One was to mention blood sports at all. The other was to contrast myself to another Boston writer, who had retired to a beautiful ranch in our corner of New Mexico, written one laudatory piece, then left for Santa Fe. Shortly after he moved, he wrote and published in Boston an article denouncing the people of Catron County. It reinforced every stereotype easterners have of the west. He wrote: "In one of Reserve's two bars the cowpokes duke it out regularly Friday and Saturday nights, toppling tables and chairs. They're often egged on by young rodeo queens, tough-looking types with leathery faces, thin lips and bouffant hairdos. The queens gravitate to the winners. 'You sure were tough tonight, Billy Joe. Let me tend your hand.'"

This was bad enough, but his attitude toward his neighbors was even worse. "I came back from town one day to find my dog's ankle pierced by what looked to have been a .22. Angry, I went to my neighboring ranch to determine what happened. 'I suspect he was chasing the B Bar cattle,' said the ranchman. 'You know what happens out here when dogs bother cattle.' "

"They get shot. And often justifiably, because dogs sometimes attack and kill or maim cattle. But my gentle dog was, I'm sure, merely chasing and barking at them, as he frequently did, and I'm sad to think he'll always limp."

While I believed that the writer felt threatened, I found it hard to recognize my home in his words. Had he lived all his life in Boston without seeing a bar fight? Were the women in Reserve really "leathery"? Certainly the ones in Magdalena weren't. Did he really think that those guns he hated were for use on humans? There'd been one shooting in Magdalena in all the time we had lived there, and it wasn't fatal—a better record than Boston or Cambridge could claim. Did he think that a dog caught chasing stock in western Massachusetts would get any different treatment than his did in New Mexico?

I was angry, but kept my remarks mild, pointing out that Catron and Socorro counties were the most friendly places I had ever lived in. I commented, maybe too snidely, that he and his dog now lived in Santa Fe where they could be safe from New Mexicans. And thought no more about it.

The next week *Impact* ran a photo of me sitting at my place in the Golden Spur Bar. Over it was a bold headline, "Disowning Stephen Bodio," and a letter that read in part, "As writers and former New Englanders, we hasten to disown the likes of Stephen Bodio—lest New Mexicans think that New England is dumping its refuse in our state, let me make clear that Bodio is an exception. It is incomprehensible that one who boasts of having the creativity to be a writer can wallow in the barbaric pastime of murdering other creativity. . . . The barbarity of his hatred of [the writer]

. . . is matched only by the relish with which he describes hunting dove and deer, in his enjoyment of 'cooked blood, hot and sweet' and his devotion to cockfights. . . ."

I was far more stunned than I should have been; it was the first time I had ever been attacked in print. In my reply I tried to stay cool: "I express no hatred of [the writer]—we have a few acquaintances in common, all of whom allege that he is a charming man and a good writer. I have no quarrel with these statements, although I do think that describing his neighbors as 'binge drinkers' is a little unkind, and that publishing these comments 1,500 miles away lacks a certain amount of professional courage. Mostly I disagree with his assessment of rural New Mexico and its hospitality—surely a legitimate subject. . . . About 'cooked blood, hot and sweet,' these are rural New Mexican delicacies prepared at any pig butchering. 'Hot' contains chiles; 'sweet' raisins. He apparently thinks I'm engaging in some sort of grim poetry rather than describing something he might encounter if he knew anyone outside of the cities."

But to my utter joy I needn't have bothered defending myself. In the intervening week a flood of letters poured in from New Mexicans, praising us and attacking the letter writer. A typical one came from a woman in Albuquerque who had seen my antagonist's denunciation first: "My feeling was, what would a transplanted Bostonian know about living in the West . . . it's with great pleasure that I say to Mr. Bodio that he truly knows what it's like to live in this wonderful state."

"See?" said Betsy. "You worry too much. I told you the home folks would be on your side."

The article somehow confirmed our place. We were now "the" writer and—even more integrated—"the" reporter. I suppose she cut a mildly eccentric figure: hacking jacket, coyote buckle, streaky ash-blonde hair blowing across her face, perpetual Camel bobbing in her mouth as she wrote down the facts in her spiral notebooks. But people asked us for favors now. When Marshall Larry Cearley's baby came down with a rare form of cancer, Betsy, media-wise, became one of the two organizers of the benefits and television coverage the town arranged to help Larry and Janet pay their staggering bills. And when the baby died despite all the agonizing effort, we attended our first Magdalena funeral. Shortly thereafter, the new school superintendent asked us if we wanted to attend a curriculum advisory meeting. We were amazed, flattered, and a little appalled. For the first time in our lives we had become respectable.

That Christmas we made our last trip back together, a totally idiotic one, by bus. Betsy had never taken one and thought it would be "fun." We stood all the way to Amarillo, where we almost got off and flew back; then progressed through a series of events including four sleepless nights, a broken heater that let the toilet (and the passengers) freeze solid, two singing kids who kicked the seat back behind us in rhythm with their songs, and a deserter who kept hiding every time we came into a station. At the Boston terminal it was snowing and they had lost our baggage, containing all our winter clothes, our travelers checks, and our presents for the families. When I objected and demanded that they find our stuff they told us that it was Christmas Eve, that they couldn't do anything, and that if I didn't shut up they would put me in jail. We flew back three days later, heartily homesick. We drove into town, seeing a cowboy in a cutting horse suit, and a drunk on the street. Betsy turned to me, grinned, and drawled, "It shore is strange when a Yankee lady from China only feels at home when she sees working cowboys and drunk Indians."

IX

The usual yard snake appeared in the spring of 1986 but even the successful extrication of it from the doghouse failed to cheer me. Looking back, it's hard to see why I was blue, but the record is there in print. At this time I wrote to the Steve and Kathe Grooms: "I have spent two months being both physically sick and mentally depressed and unable to do anything but worry and worry Bets . . . know nothing about alcoholism; have trouble considering any behavior a disease . . . but decided that my booze was hurting, not helping, my efforts to stay undepressed and so haven't had a drink in two months. [Depression] is called by others writer's block. It is horrible, and I find that naming it gives it even more power. So I don't, and endeavor to stay undepressed with doses of early rising, hours at the writing table, long walks, black tea, and mild cigars." Betsy tried to cheer me, and sometimes succeeded. Other times I felt that my unease was catching and of course that made me feel even worse. Her cheerfulness was so fundamental that any erosion of it by my own stupidity seemed a crime against nature.

Two odd things, or rather one, repeated, had been troubling my dreams that spring. I had picked up two books off the shelf in an Albuquerque bookstore: Peter Matthiessen's *Nine-Headed*

Dragon River, an autobiographical essay on Zen Buddhism, and T. S. Matthews' *Jacks or Better*, a literary memoir of the twenties. I had gotten the first because of my admiration for most of Matthiessen's writing, the second because of an interest in Robert Graves, a major character, and because Bets had enjoyed an earlier book of Matthews', *Name and Address*.

I didn't much care for either. Matthiessen's book was about Buddhism for Buddhists and I found it impenetrable; Matthews' was beautifully done but full of some of the most unpleasant literary *poseurs* I had ever encountered in fact or fiction. But they had one thing in common: each contained a loving, agonizing description of watching the narrator's wife die of cancer.

I cannot say why these portraits troubled me, but they did. They formed the unspoken subtext of unease in my letter to the Grooms, and I actually nagged Betsy into going to Bob Markwell to have a mole she had had all her life looked at. It was, of course, harmless. In the middle of one of June's hot dusty endless nights I touched my left hand between her bare shoulder blades as she slept. "Don't die," I whispered.

She fumbled for my hand. "Don't worry, I'll be with you. . . ." The end of her sentence evades me, no matter how I reach for it. "As long as I can?" "For a long time?"

All this was on my mind when I asked again: "Marry me, love?"

We were drinking, watching television, and reading, and she answered abstractedly, "Sure, why not? *What?*"

"You said 'yes,' you said 'yes,' damnit! I've got you this time! You've always been a woman of your word. You can't back down this time!"

"All right, all right. But I get to say when."

"C'mon, don't say ten years. I may not live that long."

"How about next year? But I don't know where. Here? There? I suppose you want a big party?"

"The works. Every lunatic we know, coast to coast."

"Oh, my. And I suppose you want it Catholic?" Religion had, oddly, become a subject we discussed more and more. We had started to go occasionally to San Miguel, the mostly Spanish Catholic church in Socorro. We had once attended services at the Episcopal church, but Betsy had left in a fury when a polyester-clad parishioner advised her that we'd find "a better class of people" in Socorro than in Magdalena. "The day that fat little shit is good enough to talk to Chubby Torres will be a cold day in Hell."

"I'd prefer it."

"You know that will mean all kinds of dreary paperwork. Don't worry, don't, I wouldn't have it any other way. Just don't ask me to go over to Rome. My father would be too disappointed."

Meanwhile, Chubby and Shirley had by outrageous, and ultimately self-defeating, underbidding been hired to run a Forest Service fire lookout on Grassy Mountain in the San Mateos. As they couldn't be there all the time without relief, they asked us to be their backup. The resulting once-a-week commute, the only "job" I ever had in New Mexico, actually cost us money. Two years later, no longer cursing, I have to admit it was both fun and funny.

Grassy Lookout is a glass box in the sky, standing on a stone foundation looking south over the great gaps of East and West Red Canyon. Their heads join at about eight thousand feet, still two thousand feet below the tower. As I approached the first time, I dropped down a little from the ridge, grown up in ponderosa and fir, to an open meadow where elk grazed. Beyond the canyon's abyss loomed the blue and brown bulk of Apache Peak and the Apache Kid Wilderness, thirty-by-thirty miles in area, without even the dirt forest roads that service the northern half of the San Mateos.

And what roads they were. From Magdalena to Grassy was perhaps forty miles as the raven flies, over sixty on dirt roads that started treacherous but flat and ended up in the endless mountain switchbacks over Rosedale and Cyanide Creek, where we blew at least one tire every trip in or out. I liked walking around the tower but hated both the commuting and its inevitable blowouts and the sitting the work entailed. Still, we laughed between tire changes, listened to the radio chatter, and plotted positions on minor smokes. Then, one afternoon, the dogs Sass and Maggie didn't come in.

At first they had been appalled by both the freedom and the openwork metal stairs on the tower. The one drove them in toward the base, groaning for our sympathy; and the other made them hesitate with their front paws on treads. They had seldom seen steps of any kind, much less transparent ones. But soon the impetuousness inherent in their lineage had them climbing with ease, circling the catwalk, and hunting the far edges of the meadow for such small game as green towhees and various woodpeckers. The circling that seems to be fixed in good spaniels, whether by instinct or training, kept them checking back every few minutes. At least that's the way it went for the first few weeks. Then, at about three p.m. one day, we realized they had been out of sight for an hour.

"Where do you suppose they've gone?" Betsy was always more attuned to the dogs.

"Oh, probably just treeing those turkey poults. They'll be back." Much as I thought I loved my dogs, their obsessiveness and ability to ignore shouted commands while on a hot trail often annoyed me. But something in Betsy's uneasiness prompted me to descend and circle the cliff-edge meadow, calling to the canyons below. Nothing. I walked the mile to the trail's junction with the main road, still calling. Surely they'd be along this stretch, rich with songbirds and turkeys and cottontails, I thought. But no wiggling, jingling dogs appeared. I walked back, telling myself that they'd be waiting when I got to the tower. Yet a feeling I would come to know well was forming in the vicinity of my lungs, making me gasp for air, making my heart beat faster than normal in a horrible rhythm: gone, gone, gone, lost, lost, lost. . . .

They weren't there, of course. They weren't in the oaks at the bottom of East Red Canyon, two thousand feet below, either. And when I climbed out of the bottom, they still hadn't returned, though it was near dusk and time to leave.

We were of two minds. Betsy thought she should stay to greet them if they returned while I went down to the village to gather reinforcements for the search. I argued that they probably would not return. I couldn't believe that they knew the terrain very well, and I have always nurtured a deep pessimism about dogs' psychic ability to home—indeed, about most mysterious powers. Besides, our home number was on their collars, and I thought that Betsy, with her game leg, should stay by the phone while I searched. So we descended through the switchbacks in the falling light, calling at every turn. By the time we reached the bottom I was, to my shock, nearly in tears. I had accepted the dogs as a sometimes useful, sometimes entertaining, often annoying given in my life and was shaken to realize that I felt as if two singular children were gone. I kept remembering hunts, laughs, even disasters, such as the time Mag ran full tilt into a car and smashed her jaw and had to spend two months in a muzzle, eating liquid gruel and attempting to retrieve through it. I found myself praying silently.

When we got home I called the Forest Service, and the dispatcher agreed to tell all the lookouts and work crews about the dogs. Betsy began calling the ranches that surround the high country of the northern San Mateos. There are about six. The mountains form a north-south spine about sixty miles long, with descending ridges and canyons running east and west to the grasslands below. They range from an altitude of perhaps six thousand feet on the plain and in the canyon bottoms to about ten thousand on the highest peaks. No pavement touches them, and the only permanent habitations that come close are those six huge ranches. Natural barriers made it unlikely that the dogs would have headed into the true wilderness of the southern range, but that still left us with about one thousand square miles of terrain inhabited by (maybe) twenty people, with jeep access at best.

Worse followed. The next day the sun never came out but filtered down dimly through a dense fog. One of New Mexico's rainy season storms had come. It was the most freakish weather I had seen in five years, with clouds stuck on the peaks, invisible even after the low fog in the village had burned off. A check with the dispatcher revealed that all work crews and lookouts were being pulled out for the duration of the storm, which they expected to last a week.

I borrowed a monster 4WD pickup from Rudy, knowing that

when dirt roads turned to grease the little Datsun would simply slide sideways off the mountain. Floyd agreed to come along.

That day we saw wonders. With visibility in the high country down to about thirty feet, we rounded a corner to find a bull elk— bigger than a horse, dripping black and chestnut in the eerie gray light—facing us in the middle of the road. For a moment he seemed inclined to dispute our right to exist; then he tossed his velvety rack over his shoulders and galloped up a slope that I would have had to climb on my hands and knees.

We saw turkeys, perhaps fifty, mostly mothers with poults from the size of quail to that of chickens. We saw mule deer holding on the roadsides, swiveling ears in disbelief that men could be so close. We descended a sheer drop on the side of East Red Canyon toward what looked like a roaring river, the truck slipping toward the outside edge. ("Floyd, we can't do this! I wouldn't try it with a mule," I moaned. "Well, we can't back up," was his only reply.) We got to the bottom, the truck churning through the storm of watery mud like a paddle wheeler, and emerged on the other side. Then we walked, calling, for miles, up into the Apache Kid Wilderness, and returned the same way. It rained the entire time.

On the other side of the divide, in West Red Canyon, we came to a grassy bottom that held more elk than I had ever seen, though I had hunted elk there for several years. They drifted away from our sideslipping vehicle uneasily but without haste. Several cows flowed over a wire fence along the stream with movements that were abrupt yet more graceful than a trained jumper's. I was in some sort of euphoria, despite my fears and the void in my chest that I couldn't quite fill with air.

Far above the herd, after walking and calling for another few miles, we found a single canid footprint near where I had been the day before. No dogs answered, and when we emerged onto the pavement north of the mountains at dusk, we ran out of gas. It was a long six-mile walk home.

On the third morning Betsy said, "I'm coming. Today we'll find at least one." I murmured something negative through a haze of exhaustion and arthritic knee pain. "Have faith," she said, smiling. That day we retraced the route in the truck of Chubby Torres. Betsy insisted on checking the lookout itself, despite my skepticism. We sat in the cold fog with the motor running, watching the tower appear and disappear. "Nothing here," I announced, but Chubby was staring. "I hear barks." I made another mutter of disbelief, but now Betsy was saying, "Listen."

I stepped out of the pickup to hear better, and suddenly Sass came into focus out of the fog. She was wriggling and apologizing as only a guilty spaniel can, punctuating her apologies with loud woofs, for she was not at all sure that we were us. I bundled her into the truck and into my coat, with tears of joy running down my face. I had not known how much I loved the dog. For her part she was inclined to apologize, maybe something like, "Did I really deserve that for chasing turkeys?" Betsy was grinning, just a little smug.

So when she said, "Tomorrow, Mag," I was a little more inclined to believe her. Sure enough, as soon as we reached the tower on the next day, Maggie waddled from behind it. She was juggling a months-old deer shinbone, wagging, utterly unapologetic, with an attitude of, "Boy, were you guys lost."

On the way back down Chubby suddenly announced, "This day would be perfect if I could just see a bear. This canyon is where a bear lives." We rolled around a corner, and there, bucketing down the road with its shimmering coat slipping and sliding on its fat, was a huge black, a final gift of grace. Mag wanted to chase it.

On September 2, Betsy woke me, coughing. Her niece, Carole, had been with us for a week, chain smoking, so I didn't think much of it. Still, it was an awful cough, a sort of hollow whoop. "I knew I was going to be sick," she muttered. "I've felt awful for days, as though something was going to happen."

For the next four days I tried to stick close and do all the housework. She coughed monotonously, rhythmically, and sometimes apologetically. "I've really got to quit smoking" was a phrase I heard more than once. On the fifth she said, "Go. Dove season's been open for ten days and you haven't been out once. I will not be responsible."

I drove to an odd spot, the dry Rio Salado's crossing on the Riley road, twenty-six bumpy miles north of the pavement, and started down the sandy bottom. Little pools that might conceal an early teal alternated with green waterless curves lined by willows and feathery tamarisk. I flushed several quail but saw no doves.

Two miles south of the track I came around a bend to see hundreds of ravens sitting on the smooth, bare sand. They flushed, calling and flapping, until they snagged a thermal, and then went up as if they were in an elevator, croaking and swirling in a dozen separate circles, making spirals like van Gogh's *Starry Night*. I watched, head back, mouth open, until I was dizzy. Staring into the blue void with its scattering of whirling black specks, I felt as though I were about to look through something.

A few birds cut around below, unable or unwilling to find the rising air. They cruised past, the "plop, plop, hissss" of their wings in the still air clearly audible, their glittering little eyes and open panting beaks as uncannily visible as in an acid hallucination. After a little while there were only two calling uneasily to each other, high above the breaks, shuttling back and forth in front on the blank bulk of Ladron. The others had vanished straight up.

I went home terrified. A lone raven is supposed to be a bad omen, more than one good. But this had been a vision of more ravens than I had ever seen in my life, and I was scared.

On the tenth, Bob Markwell tapped the x-ray with a pencil. "I don't like the way this looks. See that white area there?" We looked, seeing nothing as unambiguous as the line across her ribs the two years before. "It could be some sort of tumor. I wouldn't get too excited. Treatments are getting better all the time. But I think you better get a bronchoscopy in Albuquerque."

I walked around in a state of shaking clarity for two days, and argued on the phone with the office staff of the first specialist we had consulted, who had gone to a convention in Hawaii. Finally I pulled strings through a dog breeder I knew who taught pathology at the hospital, and got the papers and x-rays transferred to another specialist.

We are sitting in an office with the second specialist, a neat man with prematurely gray hair.

"It's what we call a large cell carcinoma. It's all around the top of the lung."

We sit, avoiding each other's eyes. Okay, we can deal with this.

Betsy: "Will I get better? Is there any treatment?"

A long pause. Then, softly, earnestly, taking pains to look each of us in the eyes: "No."

I reach out blindly. She reaches for me, a small figure, in a huge purple sweater she has worn for a week, despite the summer's lingering heat. She rests her head on my shoulder lightly, for just a moment, then turns toward the doctor, still holding me.

"You must have the hardest damn job in the world."

We had two more months, and there are still a few stories I must tell you.

She was in very bad shape—toughness can hold things at bay too long. She went into the hospital the next day, as we made plans together to fight with all we had.

We had to decide where to go. Boston had world-renowned specialists, and family, who of course wanted us to fly out immediately. In shock, we listened, and sent all of our goods back in a U-Haul truck with Tom McIntyre. Then we thought about it.

"This is ridiculous," said Betsy.

"I know."

"This is home, not there. If I'm going to die, I'll die here. Besides," she added grinning, "all our relatives are richer than we are. Let them fly."

Then came the matter of the Death and Dying Workshop. An earnest young intern wanted us to join one, feeling it would help us "deal with the idea of mortality." I fumbled along politely and said that neither of us had been convinced that jogging and avoiding cigarettes would guarantee our immortality. The intern was immovable. Then Betsy, who had been lying back against the pillow, looking half-asleep, raised her hand. The doctor turned.

"Young lady," she said with an imperious timbre she rarely used—full WASP consonants, bugled vowels—"I was not born in a group. Stephen and I do not make love in groups. And I will be damned if I'm going to die in a group. Thank you."

Three days after her diagnosis the x-ray on her left lung whited-out with pneumonia and the hospital rushed her onto a respirator in the intensive care unit. Here another undiscovered advantage of New Mexican ways versus that of more formal areas came out; I was allowed, even encouraged, to stay with her always, and soon started a routine of commuting each morning at seven a.m. from the Cancer Center apartment down Lomas Boulevard to the hospital, where I would bring a cup of coffee to her room and do editorial work all day. Many of the patients in the unit lay all day watching television; Betsy filled six yellow legal tablets with conversation, query, and black humor.

Her mood remained determinedly cheerful during the day. "You may entertain! I propose to do nothing." "I am too tired to write; I'm going to type. Want Apple II please." "I hope to live long enough that everyone I have met here learns I have a nice voice and a fairly graceful mode of motion. I do for some odd egotistical reason." She described me in an aside to a nurse come to do an oxygen stick, "That's my child husband."

But it was no television hospital show. Pages and pages of the tablets are taken up with details of suction, radiation, bedpans, arterial blood samples—as I look at these pages for the first time in two years, I see to my horror that one is splashed with a six-inch smear of blood. How the hell did that happen? But even here, humor creeps in: "Steve is the only man I know who would introduce a lady on a bedpan." "That big Russian bear word 'bedpan,' now what other word than 'bedpan' would wake a person at 5:25 a.m.?"

She was frightened at night more than in the day. "Anxious— keep light on. Keep light on, I scare easy." She was subject to depression and strange wonder. "My God, I'm still a young girl inside, inside this dying old lady." And still she worried about me. "There will be new friends." "I am such a nuisance and love you so much. Remind I am to get better and take you to wonderful places you've never heard of." To my bitterness that she had stuck with me through all these years of poverty only to be dying just as I started to "make it," a simple, "I'm glad to have seen the beginning. Don't screw it up."

She worked incessantly, worked to cough into a tube, to move her legs so they would not atrophy. She worked her own "ambu-bag" to fill her lungs as we wheeled her down to the radiation room.

Still, as we did, she listened to and told stories. Henry Bird, an Episcopal priest who was also a nephew of an old friend of her mother's and worked with Indian missions, was a constant visitor.

One morning she wrote to me in delight, "Henry Bird tells me of a conversation with a Canoncito Elder. 'I like elders,' says Henry." "How are the Canoncito Elders doing?" I asked on my pad. "Long silence. Then, 'Well, we're getting older . . .'"

The last words in the books are: "Korbel *Brut*. Only *Brut*— others are more expensive. This is the best." We planned a private party for her coming off the machine—the two of us, the nurse on duty, and an intern I will not name lest his humanity get him in trouble. When he drew out the tube she coughed, spat, wiped her mouth, and said in a voice even hoarser than her usual throaty one, "This tastes perfectly vile. I love it."

We had been told that if she could avoid pneumonia, if the radiation worked, and if the cancer did not metastasize to the brain, she could have as much as two years. The tumor had shrunk considerably from the radiation, and we dared hope a little. But a week after she had been released she turned to me in the Cancer Center apartment and said, more than a little hollowly, "I'm seeing double. You'd better take me back."

She went downhill, it seemed, in minutes. In an hour she was totally confused, thought she was in a mental hospital, thought she had Alzheimer's like Mary. She kept apologizing to me: "I know it's hard to be married to a crazy lady."

They gave her drugs, assured me she would sleep and be lucid tomorrow, finally forced me to go "home." They didn't have to tell me, though they did, that time was short.

I was at her bedside at six-thirty a.m. She was lucid as promised, but very weak.

"Am I going to die today?"

I temporized. "Not today. But things don't look too good."

"I know, I know. Don't make any long-range plans."

Most of the day was ours only. The thing she said that moved me most was simply, in a sleepy moment, "All this"—she gestured—"doesn't matter. You and me together, always."

Then, a little later. "All right, I'll try once more. But God, Stevie, I'm so tired."

Then I really did cry. "Jesus, love. Don't feel you have to stick around for me."

She said, "That's the sweetest thing you've ever said to me."

She held my hand and added, "I'm only worried about you, now. Please don't be offended. For the first time in my life, I feel maternal—not in a way that diminishes you. Are you going to be all right?" I don't remember my answer, but I remember that she smiled.

She drifted. At one point we had what I must call an almost literary discussion of immortality. As a Catholic, I can accept it intellectually, but only as a mystery. We laughed over the quote from Anthony Powell's devout Catholic friend Alick Dru. "I find such-and-such as difficult to believe as in a Future Life." But she sensed my disquiet and reached for my hand. "Don't worry. I'll see you later." And went to sleep.

Henry Bird came in, and later a Roman Catholic priest, also a friend, who gave her the last rites as she struggled to form words that never quite came, then drifted smiling back to sleep. Her oldest sister Jane flew in from Boston and arrived at nine, but we could not rouse Betsy. We finally went out, Jane to the apartment, I to a friend's house, where I was awakened by the phone in the dark November dawn. I already knew the message, but the form was odd. "Mr. Bodio? Mrs. Huntington passed away at five-thirty." I handed the phone to my friend, speechless. My first impulse was hysterical laughter at the pompous, inappropriate respectability of the form. The second was black despair that the person who would have laughed the hardest was somewhere where I could no longer tell her all the stories we would tell.

The next day dawned freezing cold, with black clouds blowing in from the west in bands, alternating an unearthly chill with golden light. On sudden impulse I asked Jane if she wanted to see Magdalena.

Jane was sixty-nine, a pacifist, a vegetarian for forty years, still Episcopalian. We often made gentle fun of her ways, but Betsy also said that Jane was what she had instead of a mother and that "I want to be Jane when I grow up." I did not know what she would make of our still-wild western town but I wanted her to see home.

Our first stop was at the Golden Spur. News had, in the way of small towns, preceded us. Steve Grayson, the owner, put down two glasses of Black Jack. "I can see you're Betsy's sister. You're sitting on her stool. That's her drink, on me." Jane knocked it back as though she had been hanging around the Spur for years, and thanked him. We pushed on to Floyd's.

As we climbed out his dogs and ours bayed around us, like Dutch's pack seven years before. Riley climbed her until his crocodile's head waved two feet above hers, delirious with joy. Floyd came out of the trailer with a "green"—that is fresh, bloody, wet—coyote hide and waded through the dogs. "You're Jane," he said in a voice roughened by emotion. She nodded, pushing Riley down. "That big dog is Betsy's 'Baby Riley.' And this is a coyote. It's the first one he killed all by himself!"

And vegetarian Jane looked at Floyd, grinning, as the pelt made greasy smears on her white Scandinavian sweater, and said: "Betsy is proud of her Baby Riley."

The funeral was back in Wellesley, where Virginia and the Bishop already lay. When she was still on the respirator Betsy had planned it in minute detail—pine box, as close to the old-fashioned Book of Common Prayer language as possible, Bach for music, arranged by her old friend Ed. The funeral director had asked me if there was anything "special" she might be buried in, and Jane, my sister Karen, and I went through all the boxes to find appropriate clothing and perhaps a piece of jewelry. We had settled on a silk blouse and tweed skirt and were looking for something more personal when Karen unfurled a magnificent pelt. "What's this?"

"A coyote. The first one Betsy's Riley ever grabbed."

"It's beautiful." It was, a huge forty-pound male, pale and golden.

"Maybe . . . no, it's too nice to put underground." I burst, embarrassed, into tears again, laughing at the same time. "Which means it has to be the right thing. Only you explain it to the funeral director and the lady priest."

As it turned out, neither presented a problem. Mr. Tunicliffe walked away pleased, smoothing the magnificent ruff. And the priest, a friend of Jane's, put the hawks and hares and hounds into her memorial speech.

Her old friend Joanne, a fellow journalist, documented the ups and downs of Betsy's career for the Boston *Globe*. The *Chieftain* remembered her with a series of quotes from townspeople. Mike Evans, our gun-dealer friend in Texas, wrote in a privately circulated memoir: "When my baby son died she was one of the few people that said something that made sense. I realized how hard that was when she was dying. I couldn't even stand to talk to her about it." But the last formal word was probably Tom McIntyre's in *Gray's Sporting Journal*: "She was schooled in the Northeast, traveled through Europe like the women who both intimidated and allured Hemingway, lost no small amount of money without ever feeling the least bitterness or rancour, became a journalist, then a breeder of rare margay cats, then met Steve, and lived, as a matter of fact, happily ever after."

On the first of December, we gathered above the town, at the edge of the mountains: Chubby and Shirley, Floyd, Larry Cearley, Dr. Bob Markwell, a few others. I had brought an envelope with a lock of her hair. Chubby built a roaring bonfire against the cold. I tossed the envelope onto the flames and said, "Born in China, schooled in New England, traveling all her life: Betsy finally found a home."

Temple, NH—Bar Mills, ME—Magdalena, NM
March 1987–December 18, 1988

STEPHEN BODIO

STEPHEN BODIO IS BEST KNOWN FOR HIS BOOKS ON NATURE AND SPORT, WHICH INCLUDE *A RAGE FOR FALCONS* AND *ALOFT*. HIS ESSAYS HAVE APPEARED IN *GRAY'S SPORTING JOURNAL*, *SPORTS ILLUSTRATED*, AND OTHER NATIONAL PUBLICATIONS. HE LIVES IN MAGDALENA, NEW MEXICO.

COVER PAINTING: *BETSY HUNTINGTON AND HER DOGS* BY RUSSELL CHATHAM. COVER DESIGN BY ANNE GARNER. BOOK DESIGN BY JAMIE POTENBERG. COMPOSED IN CENTAUR AND GRANJON BY WILSTED & TAYLOR, OAKLAND. PRINTED AND BOUND BY HUSKY BOOKPRINTERS, BRAINERD, MN.